THE SUICIDE CLUB

FLANNERY
O'CONNOR
AWARD
FOR
SHORT
FICTION

Nancy Zafris,
Series Editor

THE BEARER OF THIS CARD IS

THE SUICIDE CLUB

A MEMBER IN GOOD STANDING

STORIES BY **Toni Graham**

The University of Georgia Press

Athens and London

© 2015 by the University of Georgia Press
Athens, Georgia 30602
www.ugapress.org
All rights reserved
Designed by Kaelin Chappell Broaddus
Set in by 10.5 /14 Filosofia Regular
Printed and bound by Sheridan Books, Inc.
The paper in this book meets the guidelines for
permanence and durability of the Committee on
Production Guidelines for Book Longevity of the
Council on Library Resources.

Printed in the United States of America
15 16 17 18 19 C 5 4 3 2 1

Library of Congress Cataloging-in-Publication Data
Graham, Toni, 1945–
[Short stories. Selections]
The suicide club : stories / Toni Graham.
pages ; cm. —
(Winner of the Flannery O'Connor award for short fiction)
ISBN 978-0-8203-4850-6 (hardcover : acid-free paper) —
ISBN 978-0-8203-4851-3 (ebook)
1. Suicide—Fiction. I. Title.
PS3557.R2234A6   2015
813'.54—dc23
2014047206

British Library Cataloging-in-Publication Data available

It is preferable not to travel with a dead man.

HENRI MICHAUX

CONTENTS

ACKNOWLEDGMENTS

To my Avila siblings, Cathy, Paul, and Joan

With many thanks to:
Jon Billman
Catherine Brady
Nona Caspers
Scott Landers
Ann Marlowe
Ira Wood
Caron Knauer, steadfast and canny ally
Oklahoma State University for generously providing time and
opportunity

Grateful acknowledgment is made to the following publications, in
which the stories originally appeared:
"Belvedere," *Hotel Amerika*; "Burglar," *Passages North*; "Ash,"
Southern Humanities Review; "The Suicide Club," *Jabberwock Review*;
"Drop Zone," *Arroyo Literary Review*; "Hope Springs," *Epiphany*;
"God's Playground," *Confrontation*; "FUBAR," *The Meadow*

THE SUICIDE CLUB

GOD'S PLAYGROUND

The end and beginnings of beings are unknown.
We see only the intervening formations.
Then what cause is there for grief?

SHRI KRISHNA

When Jane McAllister wakes at 3:00 a.m., she hears a faint groaning from the closet. She knows it's the coat hangers.

The whispery moaning from the closet is neither a delusion brought on by her loneliness in Hope Springs, Oklahoma, nor a frightening spectre from the twilight zone. Rather, there is a scientific basis for the sound. Jane can now hear the murmurs of wire hangers; she has become receptive to sounds she might once have blocked out, just as canines can hear a dog whistle while their human masters cannot.

She has read that when the weight of clothing on wire hangers makes them sag, the hangers emit ultra-low-frequency sounds, deep moans and groans. Some sci-fi writer might spin a yarn about a woman who goes mad listening to coat hangers, but Jane does not feel as if she's losing her sanity. No: she feels a bit like she did when she ate peyote buttons once with her chums in college and could see and hear *everything* for a few hours—could see the molecules whirling in the surfaces of tables, could see the rich blue paint that decades before had covered the walls but was now hidden beneath several coats of white.

A twinge tugs at her abdomen, and when Jane slides a hand under her nightgown, she thinks she feels a knot there, just above and to the left of her navel. Cancer? Probably not, she decides—cancer is not a disease of her family. More likely she could have a benign ovarian cyst or a simple polyp on her colon. But what if the lump is a *fetus in fetu*, like the horrid thing she saw the other night on the Discovery Channel?

One can live her whole life without knowing that inside her body are the remains of her own monstrous twin. The TV program explained that sometimes when a woman is pregnant with twins, early in the gestation period one fetus fails to develop, but rather than being expelled from the mother's body, the stunted fetus is absorbed into the body of its twin, sometimes ending up in the abdominal cavity of the other baby. The absorbed twin has no brain but lives on as a mindless parasite, sucking life from its twin like a grotesque human tapeworm. The program depicted an eight-year-old boy who had a suspicious growth removed from his abdomen. The growth contained vestigial body parts: teeth, long black hair, flipperish partial hands and feet. The brainless growth with its long hair looked like a cross between a pile of gruesome detritus and a cannibal tribe's shrunken head.

Jane lies there for a long time in the dark, her hand passing again and again over the thickness in her abdomen. Does she feel it move? She can almost see her twin, her mindless doppelgänger, its blind eyes staring in the dark.

After breakfast, Jane goes out into the garden to water the rear lawn. The woman who lives in the house behind hers pops out her own kitchen door and calls hello. Jane nods to her. Though she wishes to be neighborly, she knows she has never been particularly adept at making small talk. She figures the neighbors are probably curious about the California transplant who lives alone, reputedly a psychologist of some kind and the only registered Democrat on her block. She imagines they might make fun of her behind her back, suspecting "overly educated" people of snootiness.

Once she has placed the sprinkler in the center of the lawn, she heads back to the house, but just before her hand touches the doorknob, Jane hears a raspy greeting from the old lady who lives next door.

"Pretty day, isn't it?"

Jane acknowledges that indeed the day is pleasant and adds, "How are you?"

"Oh, I'm fine," the neighbor says, "but we had a terrible scare with Earl."

Earl is the woman's husband, a stoic-faced man who comes and goes in a pickup truck, a ball cap shading his weathered face.

"A scare?" Jane turns to the woman, sees loneliness and fear in her expression.

"He had a heart attack," she says. "It's a merkle he's alive."

Jane knows the woman actually said "miracle." She learned this after awkwardly asking, "Excuse me?" the first few times she heard Oklahomans pronounce the word as "merkle."

"I'm sorry, I had no idea," Jane says, which is true. She has not heard an ambulance in the neighborhood recently; maybe the poor soul was stricken at the wheel of his truck. She does not ask for details, aware that she has to see clients at the clinic in half an hour.

"It's a merkle" is a phrase Jane now hears daily, a refrain that resounds in Oklahoma like an ever-present echo. In Oklahoma a miracle seems to happen every twenty minutes. If a doctor performs a medical procedure that saves a patient's life, the result is considered not the logical outcome of the treatment but rather a merkle. If a tornado highballs through the county but misses one's own house, that close call is attributed not to chance but to a merkle. One sees knots of praying people on the television news every evening, praying for a merkle for this or that terminal patient or lost cause. When the merkle fails to materialize, the faithful in Jane's new home state purse their lips and proclaim, "Everything happens for a reason." Jane opens the back door to her house, pauses, and says, "Is your husband all right now?"

"We think so," the neighbor says. "At times like this, I pray. I pray and pray."

"I hope that works for you," Jane says. She observes an instantaneous look of shock on the woman's face. Jane realizes too late that, as far as this elderly Oklahoma Baptist is concerned, she might as well have said Eat Shit and Die. She suddenly regrets the sticker she ordered from a catalogue and just this week attached to the bumper of her car: STOP PRAYING AND **DO** SOMETHING. Jane hears the woman's screen door slam.

Jane cannot help herself, she says a little prayer: *Please, please, please, not another entire day of nothing but eating disorders*. Already late for the clinic, when she approaches her car in the driveway she sees immediately that both rear tires are flat. She bends to examine one. Quite clearly the tire has been slashed. She wonders who would slash her tires and whether it was simply random vandalism. But then she sees that the rear window of her car has been soaped, and scrawled in soap letters is a crude 666. She has apparently been designated the neighborhood Antichrist. The stop-praying-and-do-something sticker has been revised by a black marker to read **START** PRAYING AND **DO** SOMETHING. If the sticker was intended to send a message to the community, the sticker revision and the sixes have sent her a return message: We don't want your kind here. Rather than praying for a miracle, she calls triple-A.

Jane sits in the waiting area of the service station while her car's rear tires are replaced, thinking that one thing she truly appreciates about Oklahoma is that—unlike San Francisco—it still has full-serve stations. Not only do uniformed attendants rush out to pump the gas and wash the car's windows, but they actually offer to vacuum out the car, gratis. Each time she drives into a gas station here, she has the pleasant feeling of being in a time warp. She remembers sitting in the backseat of her family's old Buick, smelling the intoxicating fumes of Shell, listening to her father chat with a white-capped attendant while hearing in the background the bonking sounds of heavy glass Coca-Cola bottles being released from coolers in the station.

After her car is outfitted with two new tires, Jane pulls the vehicle into the full-service aisle to get some gas. The attendant who pumps her gas gives her a strange look as he gestures at the 666 on her back window and calls out, "Can I wash that off for you?"

"Please," she replies, forcing a smile and offering no explanation. As he scrubs off the numerals, he spies the "I ♥ San Francisco" frame around the license plate and approaches the driver's side window, asking, "Are you from California?"

"Born and bred," Jane says, then feels herself flush at the word "bred," which seems a bit graphic.

"Were you ever attacked by birds?"

For a moment, Jane does not know how to reply to this astonishing inquiry. Finally she simply answers, truthfully: "I was viciously pecked in the head once by a huge black bird—a starling or a crow. I guess I was too near its nest."

He nods, and Jane suddenly gets it. The guy must have seen Hitchcock's *The Birds* on Turner Classics. He has no concept of what California is like, other than from movies and TV. To him, Jane's home state is an alien land where savage avian attacks can happen anytime.

When Jane arrives home from the clinic, exhausted by six hours of bulimics, she catches a glimpse of herself in the hallway mirror and is startled. Her face is simultaneously familiar and strange, and she pauses to look more closely. Maybe it's just the hair, she figures—her hair is today giving her a strange appearance. In an attempt at frizz control, she became carried away with the flat iron, and now her hair is overly straight and sticks out at the bottom in an artificial manner. Her hair is balky even at its best, but in its fried-straight mode today, it looks like the hair one sometimes sees on African American women: coarse, artificially broomstraw straight, the ends sticking out from overuse of hot combs.

She sees that she looks a bit wild-eyed. Has she taken too much decongestant, or did she accidentally double up on her hormone tablets?

Only two days ago she saw a program about wild-eyed zombies in Haiti. The camera followed two live humans, lurching across the television screen, who were described by the narrator as zombies—not as "so-called zombies" or "zombie-like," but flat-out zombies. Her hand stilled on the remote control when she heard that one. Zombies, weren't they mythical creatures or figments? Why was the word "zombie" coming from the mouth of a network journalist? It seemed there were people in Haiti who died, were buried, but later came up out of their graves and walked among their neighbors, with vacant, dark-pupiled stares in their eyes, living but not quite with us. Do zombies breathe? Are they spirits, per se? Jane knows that the Latin word for "breath" is *spiritus*, so to be a spirit is in fact to breathe.

The program informed viewers that there was some basis in reality for the zombie phenomenon. Local witch doctors created the zombies to serve their own needs. First the medicine man chose a victim to poison—usually a local miscreant of some sort, a thief or an adulteress. After the wrongdoer was publicly excoriated for the crime, the shaman secretly administered a potion, one that immediately propelled the victim into a coma so deep it mimicked death. Tetrodotoxin extracted from the puffer fish was so virulent that, with a very low dose, the poisoned person was instantly paralyzed. This much Jane can easily believe, as she herself has twice been poisoned by something as benign as swordfish consumed in a tony restaurant. Each time, she ate a fresh and tasty seafood meal, but within hours she fell suddenly asleep, actually slumping over, laying her head down and falling into a deep slumber, like the guests at the party in *Sleeping Beauty*.

Shortly after his victims were buried, the Haitian witch doctor would return in the dark to the graves and exhume them. More often than not, the victims were still alive, remaining comatose. A couple of days later they would wake, stand, and walk, often with a vacant look in their eyes. As with other forms of suspended animation—be it from freezing in an ice pond or from cardiac arrest—loss of oxygen to the brain often resulted in damage to that organ. Some of the dug-up sinners returned to their communities, chastened and nicely frightened into compliance, but others were little more than dead bipeds on the move.

Toward the end of the month, Jane usually finds herself in the local Walmart. When she runs out of money, she economizes by shopping here, though she dislikes buying from this megachain. She takes out her checkbook to pay for a box of Sudafed, after first signing a form as if she were some sort of registered sex offender. Oklahoma, per the recent national trend, has outlawed over-the-counter sale of pseudoephedrine, one of the meth-cooking ingredients. One now has to face down the pharmacist and go on record before being allowed to relieve her own nasal congestion. After she writes a check, the amount appears on a lighted display above the cash register, along with the flashing words *Waiting on approval*. She cannot help herself, she points to the lighted letters and says to the pharmacy associate, "That sign is incorrect. It should say waiting *for*, not waiting *on*." The clerk simply stares at Jane, his facial expression flickering between disinterest and malice.

Now the store's PA system blares forth: "Surprise Dad with new power tools for Father's Day! Our biggest sale of the year is taking place right now!" Oh, sweet Jesus, next Sunday is Father's Day. If Valentine's Day was once the most painful day of the year, this has now changed for the worse. All one needs for a really, really swell Father's Day is for one's own father to have committed suicide. Not only is she reminded again, as she is in some manner every day, that she no longer has a father, but there are of course the unspoken words from her father's grave: I'd rather be dead than stay alive for a daughter like you.

As she leaves the pharmaceuticals department, Jane passes the greeting card section, where clumps of shoppers, primarily women, huddle around the Father's Day cards, reaching over each other's heads to select exactly the right message for dear old Dad.

Jane is bushwhacked by a devastating memory of something long forgotten. She sees herself as she was then, in her twenties, not yet married, browsing through racks of Father's Day cards. An attractive man was standing next to her, also looking at cards, and Jane said, "Gee, it's hard to find the right Father's Day card when you can't stand your father." The man laughed appreciatively and gave her an appraising glance, and Jane blushed, proud of her irreverence. Even then, she was well on her way to becoming a Goneril or Regan, one of Lear's bad daughters. And had not her father indeed gone blind like Lear, and had he not gone mad? Would it have killed her to be more like Cordelia, a better daughter—could she not have troubled herself to buy a loving Father's Day card for the man who sired and supported her? But no, she was too busy being a rebellious little shit, too busy making what she thought were witty remarks as she flirted.

"Show Dad how much you care!" the PA system now exhorts.

She notices that she is shuffling from the bedroom to the kitchen. Yes, I *shuffle*, she acknowledges, listening to the swish-swish of the soles of her slippers as she slides like a geriatric case along the hardwood floors on the way to the stove for another cup of coffee. Christ, she does not even have the spirit to pick up her feet.

At the table, she flips to the obits as is her daily habit. She often jokes that her Irish blood drives her to do so: her mother always wryly referred to the obituaries as "the Irish sports page." In any case, Jane can count on the newspaper to get her up to speed on who is still left on this earth and who has been recently added to the mounting pile of corpses that signifies her passage through middle age. When she was young, she never understood why her parents and grandparents indulged in major lamentations every time some superannuated matinee idol or has-been crooner dropped dead, but now she understands all too well.

The obits in Oklahoma publications are particularly strange, Jane finds. Seldom is the cause of death reported—which, other than the age of the deceased, is the most relevant information. No, rather than the cause of death, what is reported here is the church affiliation of the deceased. But of course, no one actually *dies* in Oklahoma. Jane has yet to see the word "died" in an obit in this state of the Union. Rather, what is reported is that Jim-Bob or Kyle or Misty "went to join the angels" or "was reunited with her Lord Jesus" or "sits on the lap of the Blessed Savior." In today's local newspaper, beneath the photo of a closed-eyed infant appearing post mortem, are the words "entered God's playground."

But now in the national obituaries segment she sees an equally terrible notice. She reads that a notable jazz singer from the 1950s escaped from his deathbed in the hospital and attempted to walk home, dying on the sidewalk, three blocks from his house.

Would she not escape from any Oklahoma hospital and walk to California to die? She envisions a grotesque reenactment of the Dust Bowl migration: Jane grimly forging toward California, desperate as a Joad to escape the parched environment of Oklahoma. No hospital in the Sooner State is strong enough to keep her here to die and be buried in the red dirt of Oklahoma rather than crawl home to expire in a field of golden California poppies.

A friend of Jane's died when they were both barely girls, still in their twenties. The other girl died instantly in a car crash, and Jane and the rest of the girl's friends attended the funeral. At first Jane thought the most horrible part of the event—her first funeral—was that her friend's body was present, openly displayed in a casket carried right into the temple by six boys, brothers and young friends of the deceased. But far worse was the eulogy. The bishop delivered an interminable sermon that made Jane so angry she had to restrain herself from stalking out. From the things the man said about her friend—generic platitudes—Jane could tell he had not actually known the girl, perhaps never even met her, which was certainly no surprise, as her friend had detested the family's religion. But rather than talking about her friend or even about loss and how to deal with grief, the bishop spent close to an hour expounding the doctrine that, according to the Book of Mormon, the entire family would be reunited in the afterlife, reunited in both spirit and body. It seemed her friend's parents actually believed the whole family's decayed bodies would miraculously reconstitute themselves and—presto, change-o!— turn up in the afterlife so the family could hang out together as if nothing had ever happened. She ground her teeth throughout the sermon, unable to prevent herself from mumbling whispered phrases every so often: *Get real, Rev* and *In your dreams!*

But she now cherishes the same dreams. It is true that since Mom and Sarge passed on, she can for the first time in her life accept the concept of her own death, and solely because she looks forward to being reunited with her parents and grandparents. In fact, blood seems truly to be thicker than water when it comes to the sweet hereafter, because Jane has not found herself continuing to miss her dead young friend. No, she just wants to see her parents again, the same parents she spent much of her life trying to get away from.

And, Mormonesque, she wants their bodies to be there, too—no ghostly ectoplasm for this gal. She wants the Other Side to be like the home movies that her family used to watch on Christmas mornings. In those black-and-white films, Mom was still a beautiful young woman in a short dress, with long, slim legs and genuine alligator pumps. Her father was then a man with forearms like anvils, and not from working with a personal trainer or rowing machines in a twenty-four-hour gym for narcissistic boys. No, her dad's biceps, round and hard as coconuts, came from hard work, and his beautiful white teeth came from his parents, both of whom had full mouthfuls of straight white teeth when they went to their graves. Unlike Jane's former husbands, Sarge never had to bleach his teeth or invest in porcelain veneers.

The first time in her childhood that she had what might be termed a philosophical discussion with her father was the day following Hemingway's death. Still reading Nancy Drew mysteries at that age, she had certainly not yet read any of Hemingway's work, but the author's face was ubiquitous and his exploits well known. Jane was accustomed to seeing the man's white-bearded face just about everywhere: frequently on the cover of *Life* magazine, in newsreels at the Sunday matinees, on TV documentaries on the family's black-and-white RCA. Jane's mother was still in the shower that morning while Jane and her father were perusing the newspaper together at the breakfast table, Sarge reading the sports page first, Jane feeling adult and sophisticated as she tented the front page of the *Chronicle* in front of her plate the way she had seen her grandfather do, even though she was reading only the comic strips. She had asked for some coffee, too, but her father just gave her a sour look and set a glass of milk near her plate.

There he was again, that writer guy with the bushy white beard, grinning at Jane from the front page of the newspaper, holding a rifle. She was brought up short by the headline.

"Dad," she said, "Ernest Hemingway was killed in an accidental shooting."

She was shocked by her father's rude laughter. "It was no accident," her father said, shaking his head.

"But it says—"

"I don't care what the paper says," Sarge said. "He's a very proficient marksman, an experienced hunter. He obviously killed himself, the coward."

Stunned, Jane said nothing for a few moments, then said, "Even if that's true—that he killed himself—I don't think that means he's a coward."

"You don't know what you're talking about." Sarge's voice rose angrily. "People who do that are afraid to face life—they're yellow."

Jane has once again plopped herself in front of the television—a sad state of affairs, she knows. But she has yet to rustle up much of a social life in Hope Springs, and the town offers little in the way of entertainment or recreation for those beyond college age—that is, until people are ready to be shuttled over to the town's "assisted living center." A year and a half more before she can leave Hope Springs behind. When she agreed to come into the last two years of a four-year NIMH grant, not as a principal but as a consultant, she committed to stay the course for the entire two years of her clinical work in the university drop-in clinic. She is stuck.

Her evenings for the most part now consist of reading, reviewing notes she has made about clinic clients, or watching TV. As she looks under the pillows on her bed for the remote control, she thinks about the fact that no man has walked through the door of this bedroom—if one does not count the semi-toothless workman who came to install the plantation shutters—much less slept in this bed, since she moved to Hope Springs. Could this be the beginning of the end? She did not realize during the last love affair she had in California that the romance might indeed be the "last" love affair.

She looks at a man on the TV screen, a handsome actor in a network drama. His hair is blue-black, his haircut impeccably stylish. His flawless masculine jaw and cleft chin exhibit the perfect degree of five-o'clock shadow; his teeth are impossibly white, and when he smiles, dimples appear. His face says East or West Coast just as much as the Hope Springs males' faces scream Oklahoma. As she stares at the actor, she becomes aware that she is actually drooling! Spit has not only trickled out of the corner of one side of her mouth but is making its way down her chin like a wayward tear.

She would like a relationship or "dates," surely, but how is this possible in Hope Springs? The men here share only two types of faces among them. Type 1 men wear a ball cap, from which scraggly, mullet-like hair escapes in the back. The faces of Type 1 guys are sun-hardened, ruddy, furrowed by years of cigarettes and/or pooched out in one cheek by chewing tobacco. Type 1 men have rumbly voices and phlegmy-sounding laughs, and when they do laugh, one sees they are missing multiple teeth.

Type 2 men have faces one sees on TV news anchors in Oklahoma and on one's affluent dentist or a neighbor who is a high school teacher. These men look like adult babies, their faces round and smooth, blank or vacantly smiling, their expressions as devoid of complexity as the face of a cooing infant. Type 2 is the face of the "Christian" family man, the man who takes his family to church every Wednesday night and twice on Sunday, who watches college and even high school football on TV or churchy programs on the Trinity channel, and who hates homosexuals and demonizes abortion. Doubt seldom marks the faces of these men; they accept everything as part of God's plan.

Jane is driving across a bridge on her way to the dry cleaner, admiring the green canopy of trees lining the roadway. Summer in Hope Springs, though brutally hot, is more bearable than fall. This past autumn, she was driving over this very bridge when she noticed that the trees had uniformly lost their leaves, something that never really happened in California. She thought, *All the trees are brown*, and then, as she looked up through the windshield, *and the sky is gray*. "Oh, my god," she said aloud, nearly losing her hold on the steering wheel. I never realized, she thought, never understood the meaning of that dopey song, before now.

And of course, it *was* California-dreaming that she was doing, whether she realized it or not. For most of her life, she had simply accepted that above her were blue skies and around her green trees. Never had it occurred to Jane that one could go for months on end seeing nothing but gray skies and brown trees, but she came to realize that such drabness was exactly what was in store for her here. She felt bad, then, for thinking that motley pop-rock group in the sixties was cheesy—clearly the Mamas and the Papas had known more than she had. She was forced to pull off the road to sit and weep like a Pentecostal in the car as traffic surged past her.

Now Jane feels chilled and shivers, her teeth clacking like cartoon dentures. Homesickness is like any other illness. Your muscles and bones ache; you keep checking your temperature. You sometimes fall asleep in a chair, suddenly, as if you are narcoleptic, and when you wake up, first you do not know where you are and then, when you remember, you choke up for an instant. You shiver a lot and wear coats and jackets even in the heat of the afternoon. Your brain is as slow and congested as a hair-clogged drain.

When she stops at a red light, looming in her peripheral vision to the right is an expanse of fire-engine red, and she turns her head and looks through the passenger-side window of her car. The enormous vehicle sitting in the lane next to her waiting at the light is not a fire engine at all, but a massive Coca-Cola truck on its delivery route in Hope Springs. Seeing the truck has the impact of a thudding punch to her abdomen, and she even doubles over at the wheel. She is transported back to the early 1960s, when her young father has taken a job with Coca-Cola. He could have gone to college on the GI Bill, but he already had a family to support, and he imagined he was too old for college, too out of step with those he believed to be sissy bookworms or frat boys.

As the Coca-Cola truck makes a turn and passes from view, the red truck is replaced in Jane's mind by a mental image. On the roof of her family's tract house stands Sarge: her strong young father with his muscled arms and his crow-black hair. He embraces a crimson figure; at first glance, they appear to be a couple engaged in a tango. But Sarge's partner is a cardboard Santa, nearly as tall as he is. Santa winks an eye as he holds in one raised hand a bottle of Coca-Cola and waves the other gloved hand in a greeting to all who see him, his Coke bottle in profile like a torch against the sky. Sarge has brought the Santa home from the Coca-Cola headquarters and has climbed to the roof to place him there for the holiday season.

Now that her parents are gone—that horrible euphemism "gone"— Jane has difficulty thinking of even one negative trait either of them may have possessed. Just as, when they were alive, she was rarely able to think of anything she liked about her parents but could focus intently on their numerous transgressions against her, now she can rarely imagine either of them without first infusing them in her memory with a saintly glow and an aura of heroic beneficence. As an undergraduate in psychology, Jane first encountered the term "splitting." She recognized herself immediately as one of those who see things only as black or white, never able to perceive any shades of gray. She sees her parents now like a holy vision at a shrine. Her mother's beauty is intact, the straps of her alligator pumps wrapped around her lovely slender ankles, a red azalea corsage pinned to the lapel of her blazer for Christmas. Her father waltzes on the roof with Santa, forever young.

But her actual last image of her father is not of a young man home from the war, embracing a cardboard Santa on the rooftop. No: the last time she saw her father, he was prone on his four-poster bed, his face distorted by a plastic bag bearing the printed warning *Caution, this is not a toy*. And Sarge was playful to the very end. He had drawn an X through the calendar page for the day he took his own life, leaving a clearly legible note in his large scrawl in bold black fountain-pen ink, "I'm gone. Sayonara!"

Sunday morning follows a fitful sleep. Jane was awake again in the middle of the night, once more listening to the mournful clothes hangers in her closet. After she starts the coffee brewing, she opens the front door to retrieve the newspaper from the porch and blinks against the bright morning sun. She sees something she thinks cannot really be there but must instead be a pre-coffee trick of light: On her neighbor's front lawn is a miniature circus tent—red and green striped with a scalloped flap opening in front. A yellow banner on the top of the tent ripples in the breeze.

When they were kids, she and her brother slept in the back garden sometimes, in a little kiddie tent that Sarge pitched for them on the grass. They were delighted to carry their sleeping bags from the house, along with flashlights and bags of marshmallows, and to fall asleep outside, the garden as thrilling and foreign as an oasis in the Sahara. As for a tent on a front lawn, in San Francisco a pile of dog feces or a homeless person foraging for aluminum cans would be more likely.

A bit of motion comes into Jane's peripheral vision, and she turns to see the old man, Earl, lumbering across his front lawn, the habitual ball cap on his head, toting a plate of muffins. Earl, it seems, has rebounded from his heart attack, returned from the near-dead.

"Grandpa!" kids' voices say in unison, and from the front flap of the striped tent pop the heads of two children, a boy and a girl. Jane did not know the neighbors had grandchildren, much less owned a lawn tent, and after learning of the old guy's heart attack, she wasn't too sure she'd see him again. Earl nods to her as he approaches the kiddie tent, and he says, "Mornin' to you, ma'am." Well, hell, maybe the old gal's prayers have actually worked—maybe there has been a miracle.

After returning to her kitchen, Jane reads the obits while she drinks French roast to jolt herself awake. But she sees something through the kitchen window, a jerky movement behind the magnolia tree parallel to the driveway. Has she imagined the motion? Perhaps a squirrel has hopped from the roof, or maybe the two kids have ventured into her yard. But when she moves closer to the window and peers through the blinds, she sees there is a man in her driveway. A Type 1 man, to be precise. The man wears a Houston Oilers T-shirt stretched over his distended belly, the belly doubtless a result of huge quantities of Oklahoma's miserable 3.2 beer. The predictable mullet hangs in a ponytail behind the Oilers cap on his head. But—this is too much—she sees that in place of one of his hands, he actually has a hook. A man with a hook is loitering in her driveway as if she is living out some creepy Internet legend. She pauses, wondering whether she should confront him, call the sheriff, or simply hope he will go away. Instead she continues to peer though the blinds. She sees now that the man holds a bucket with his hook and a squeegee in his hand, like one of the guys who shake down motorists for handouts back home in San Francisco. Trepidation gives way to annoyance, and she opens the kitchen door, not even self-conscious about wearing a robe and slippers.

"What are you doing?" she says, keeping her voice devoid of emotion, just as she does in the clinic. The question is somewhat inane, as Jane can clearly observe that the man is now scrubbing the back window of her car.

"I'm cleanin' off that soaped thing on the back," he says, pausing and looking up at her with deep brown eyes, his gaze as direct as a dog's. "It ain't right."

Jane is alarmed to see that 666 has been scrawled a second time on her car's back window. She assumes the man is excoriating her and says weakly in her own defense, "Someone else put it there."

"I know that," the guy says, setting the bucket down on the driveway and releasing it from his hook. "I know who did it. It ain't right. I'm cleanin' it off for you."

Jane's first instinct is to reach for her purse, figuring he either wants a handout or requires a tip, but something keeps her from moving. No, she realizes, the guy is just trying to be nice. Cash would offend him. I really am an alien here, she realizes—in Oklahoma a cash gratuity is not always the answer. She says thank you but then hears an astonishing thing come from her mouth, as if she were a Chatty Cathy doll from her childhood and someone pulled the string to make her speak: *God bless you.* She closes the door before he can laugh at her or see her blushing.

The obits behind her, she turns to the local segment of the newspaper and is immediately bombarded with Father's Day items: local-color pieces about Oklahoma City anchorwomen and their fathers, Hope Springs's mayor and his father. The Family Living section covers a Girl Scout father-daughter pancake breakfast. A photo of the Girl Scouts and their dads covers most of one page, and she finds herself looking closely at the faces of the fathers. Looking for what? she wonders. One cannot tell from examining the grinning faces of these fathers, some of whom have their arms looped around the shoulders of their daughters, which father beats his children, which one may go on to blow his brains out or suffocate himself with a plastic bag. She sees that one father is seated between two identical girls, freckled twins to the right and left of him, mirror images of each other save for the fact that only one girl is missing a tooth.

She touches her abdomen now, recalling the night when she thought she found a thickness there and wondered if she were harboring her own replicate, a *fetus in fetu.* Beneath her fingers thrums a pulse, warm and vibrant. She is not sure whether she feels the heartbeat of a miniature twin or the throb of her own pounding heart.

HOPE SPRINGS

Even though thou seekest a body,
thou wilt gain nothing but trouble.

Tibetan Book of the Dead

Slater steps onto the front porch to scoop up the morning newspaper. When he stands, he finds himself looking up at the eaves, just above the mailbox. Only yesterday, there was a large wasps' nest there. He is embarrassed to admit to himself that he had not realized what the thing was. Living in Manhattan had not exactly made him an expert on Oklahoma entomology, unless one counted a nodding acquaintance with cockroaches. But he had received a sharply worded note from his mailman: unless he removed the nest, there would be no more home delivery.

He is so allergic to stings that he has to carry an EpiPen to avoid anaphylaxis, so he was chary of dealing with the nest himself, and he sure as hell was not about to ask his wife to do it for him. At first, when looking through the Yellow Pages for a bug-extermination service, he was unable to find any. He soon realized that the heading "exterminators" no longer existed. Bug killers were now termed "pest control" experts. Slater felt like a wuss for seeking one at all. He remembered his father going out on the back patio of their family home carrying a Louisville Slugger and, with a powerhouse swing that would make Bonds on 'roids look tame, sending a nest flying from the patio.

When the pest control van drove up yesterday morning, things grew rapidly worse: the exterminator was a woman. Slater was given the humiliating task of standing by while a petite female with a blond ponytail sprayed the nest with a can of something and then collected 125 ducats for being braver than the man of the house.

Though Slater had always thought his father was manlier than he was, he had not realized the old man was a stand-up guy until Poppy was gone. He and his sisters had often complained about what a coldhearted guy Poppy could be, and his suicide certainly seemed to confirm their opinion. Later, though, they learned that Poppy was a serial blood donor who had earned several plaques and a write-up in the Albany newspaper for record-breaking donations, that he had always given 15 percent of his income to Jewish charities, and that he had designated himself an organ donor. This last was not to be—the mandated autopsy interfered with Poppy's attempt to give part of his body to someone who needed it more than he did.

Slater and his sisters were stunned three months ago when legions of mourners showed up for Poppy's memorial service, people they had never before seen—weeping, all of them, as if these strangers themselves were Poppy's family. Droves of them approached Slater, tearful or sobbing, to tell him what a wonderful man Isaac had been, how he had chauffeured them around, cooked for them when they were sick, come to their kids' graduation ceremonies and bar mitzvahs, always weighed down with food and gifts. Their tears dried up momentarily when they began regaling Slater with tales of how funny Poppy had been, how he had been able to coax them out of their darkest moments with his good cheer and his hilarious jokes. Poppy, it seemed, was perceived by everyone but his family as a hybrid of Santa Claus, Robin Williams, and David Ben-Gurion.

Before retirement Poppy was a longshoreman, a thinking man's dockworker like Eric Hoffer. When he was young, he met Hoffer and even knew Harry Bridges, and he remained a staunch union man until the day he took his own life. Suicide or not, everyone else at the funeral seemed to have believed all along that Poppy was a mensch.

Now a lone wasp buzzes on the porch, flying frantically around the spot where the nest used to hang. The poor schmuck, thinks Slater, it went out for a while and came back to discover there has been some sort of wasp holocaust, leaving him alone in the world. Slater cannot help it, he feels bad for the creature and rather wishes he had not caved in to the mail carrier.

Back in the kitchen, he decides he would rather go out for breakfast and turns off the kettle. He knows his wife will sleep for at least another hour, so he leaves a note on the whiteboard: *Beth—Went to Sancho's—back soon.* Usually he vets students' projects on Saturday mornings before he and Beth go out for a bike ride, but he has a hankering for huevos rancheros. Granted, the eggs will be Oklahoma style, not Tex-Mex, so he knows the unmistakable flavor of ketchup will taint the dish. The "Mexican" restaurant in Hope Springs is a place called Siesta Sancho's, which has a red and green neon sign bearing a logo, the form of a man slumped against a wall with a sombrero pulled over his eyes, the prototypical racist vision of the lazy Mexican. The restaurant also sells T-shirts with the same snoozing image on the front. The shirts with the dozing, mustachioed, sombreroed Hispanic are pervasive in the town of Hope Springs.

He goes quietly into the bedroom, where Beth sleeps belly-down, breathing deeply, her gray-flecked black hair curtaining one eye, an arm flung across the spot where Slater slept. In the mornings she has begun to give off what he thinks of as a doughy smell, like sourdough bread except less appealing. Nothing that comes with aging is beautiful or fresh— this much he knows. And if Slater is repelled by his wife's yeasty smell, she has complained somewhat bitterly that he often "reeks" of garlic. Maybe her doughy smell and his garlicky smell commingle in their bed to mimic the scent of Texas toast.

Slater picks up from the floor a pair of Levi's and his Tool T-shirt and slips them on. Oh, shite, the T-shirt conjures a less-than-pleasant recollection. He wore the Tool tee on campus earlier this week, nearly late for teaching his senior seminar. While normally he would have worn at least an Oxford-cloth shirt and khakis, dressing in jeans and a T-shirt is acceptable in his department—the architecture professors never dress up the way some of the other faculty do. A few of the guys in English and in Theater are downright fops. But wearing the Tool shirt turned out to be a particularly unfortunate choice. As he rushed across the parking lot and toward the architecture building, he heard a girl, probably an undergraduate, say to her friend—not even bothering to lower her voice—"I bet he *is* a huge tool, too." Her friend laughed.

Was simply being a fifty-nine-year-old noticeably balding guy wearing a rock-band T-shirt reason enough to be considered a frickin' tool? Maybe he had heard incorrectly—maybe she actually said, "I'll bet he *has* a huge tool."

He puts on his Mets cap, glad that Beth is not awake to call him on the choice. She has often told him that most people are not fooled by the hat ploy. When she sees a man wearing a cap, she assumes the sartorial choice was made for one of only two reasons: he is very short and compensating by adding a hat, or he is bald. Well, what the fuck is he supposed to do: spray his bald spot with brown dye the way guys on TV do?

When he steps out onto the porch again, this time he notices that the neighbors have affixed yellow ribbons to the trees in front of their houses. Who are they mourning now? he wonders. He has noticed for quite some time that Oklahomans seem somehow to enjoy PDGs: public displays of grief. There is always a flag at half staff in Oklahoma, often for some dead football coach or deceased Republican former governor. Just as, during the historical Oklahoma land rush, many cheated by sneaking in early in order to claim the better homesteads, now they rush to get to the memorial services "sooner," among the first to be photographed publicly sobbing. The Sooners come in droves, bearing teddy bears and plastic-wrapped bunches of flowers, weeping and mugging for the cameras.

He guesses that huge PDG exercises are the only thing other than football championships that provide a sense of glamour here. Whether this aspect of Oklahoma culture is a sad consequence of the Oklahoma City bombing he cannot say. He and Beth came here several years after the terrible disaster at the Murrah Building. Slater was offered an endowed chair at the university, and when he reluctantly but sensibly accepted, Beth left her New York job in advertising and opened a gift shop in Hope Springs.

The yellow ribbons are perhaps Iraq related, he figures. He and Beth are antiwar blue voters, living in a red state that is gung ho about the war. He remembers the yellow-ribbon type very well from the Vietnam War days. There was always a certain sort of person who loved wearing POW bracelets, loved *war*. In Oklahoma many of those people, older now, have young adult children who wear WWJD? bracelets, expecting the entire world to believe that, every second of every day, they are wondering what Jesus would do.

Slater seats himself in Sancho's and without consulting the menu orders a pot of coffee and the huevos. He has chosen a booth in the rear of the restaurant, his back to the wall so that no one can see his bald spot. He removes his cap, then remembers he forgot to bring the newspaper. Slater habitually carries a small notebook in his jacket pocket in case he thinks of something he needs to take care of or wants to make a quick sketch. He pulls out the notebook and a pen and begins to make some notes in order to pass the time—no, face it, Slater, in order to seem occupied, to avoid looking like a sad sack.

He has recently begun to find himself making lists, lists that serve no real purpose. He compiles the lists, then seldom peruses them again. He looks at the list he began last time he jotted in the notebook.

THINGS NEVER TO DO:

1. Never answer the door to someone carrying a clipboard.

2. Never sit next to a midget on the bus.

This one is certainly moot, as he has not been on a bus since they left New York. He crosses out the word "midget" and replaces it with "dwarf." After a moment he crosses that out too and writes "little person." Then he changes it back to "midget."

3. Never trust someone who is always smiling.

Slater now adds

4. Never call a pest control service—do your own killing.

He looks up for a moment and is surprised to see walking into Sancho's the psychologist who runs the suicide survivors workshop. "Dr. Jane" they call her. He thinks her last name is something like McPhee or McMillan—it can't be McGraw, that's Dr. Phil, isn't it? Dr. Jane is the group facilitator, also a "suicide survivor." Slater has heard from friends who have been in rehab that the facilitators are always fellow addicts or fellow rape survivors or fellow something-survivors. Slater prefers the more antiquated terminology: "victim"—he and the others in the group are all victims of suicide, no matter if the word "survivor" is now the preferred nomenclature.

Dr. Jane is ordering coffee, and he cannot help but catch a good view of the back of her. She wears one of those ruffly knee-length full skirts he has been noticing on campus, but he can see that she has a nice ass for a woman her age, and her tanned legs are still shapely. He knows that when she turns toward him, she will have cute little painted toenails emerging from her sandals. He feels himself stirring like some jacked-up seventh-grader drooling over a sexy high school girl, and his face heats. He is still married to Beth, has been married to her for thirty-some years, will probably always be married, and Dr. Jane is aware he has a spouse. He pages through the notebook, not wanting her to see him staring.

She passes by his table on the way to her own, her eyes not visible behind Jackie-O sunglasses, and as she breezes by (yep, there are the red toenails), she only nods slightly, with a tiny trace of a close-lipped smile of acknowledgment. Damn—he did not realize until now that he has some sort of crush on her. He figures this is no different from the crushes students develop on their professors; he has heard about what shrinks call "transference."

Metallica's *Black Album* plays on Slater's car stereo as he drives home from breakfast. He turns up the volume even louder, the sound thumping through and from the car the way the gangbangers at home drove around, glaring out their car windows at anyone who dared to object. He presses the lever to open both front windows, treating his neighbors to a sweet taste of metal as he drives down his own block. When he pulls into the driveway, he spots a man who appears to be in his twenties, jogging along, wearing running shorts and a Siesta Sancho's T-shirt, accompanied by a Doberman. The guy slows to a walk and stares Slater down. He and the dog are both lousy with muscles.

"Got that cranked up kind of loud, huh?" the guy says. His face wears no expression: he is either naturally poker-faced or making an effort not to show his cards. Is his question a benign inquiry, or is it a challenge? Slater is not sure.

"Rock on," Slater responds.

"Sure thing, old-timer," the jogger says, then canters off.

I ought to kick his ass, Slater thinks. It is not a serious thought, but he feels the sting: *old-timer*. He has become a codger, Slater realizes, a schlemiel.

Beth is sitting at the kitchen table when Slater enters. In front of her rests a ceramic pot of what smells like mint tea, and she sips from a cup as she watches the tiny Sony tucked into a niche on one wall. "How was Sancho's?" she says, her gaze still fixed on the screen.

"Ketchupy."

Beth asks if he thinks the weather is okay for a bicycle ride, but Slater finds he has lost his zest for exercise. "Hon, would you mind? I wanted to watch the Mets game this morning, and then I need to do some prep work for the Price Tower trip." In fact, he had planned neither; he just wants some time to himself.

"Price Tower?" Her expression registers no recognition.

"Beth, I told you, I'm taking my undergrads to Bartlesville this week—a field trip to the Frank Lloyd Wright building."

She says that oh, yes, now she remembers about the Price Tower trip but then returns her attention to the TV and says, "Will you look at that, Dave?"

When Slater follows her gaze, he sees a wedding cake on the screen. Beth picks up the remote and turns up the volume.

"—entirely out of Krispy Kremes," he hears the TV person say. Apparently a woman in Muskogee is selling wedding cakes made from Krispy Kreme doughnuts. What is more notable, it seems the woman can barely keep up with the orders for wedding cakes made of doughnuts and is looking to expand her facilities. Beth laughs good-naturedly.

Slater says nothing. This is the woman with whom he occupied the administration building at Columbia during the student strikes in '68, the black-haired antiwar firebrand and fellow SDS member, the woman with whom he expected to be arrested. But on the evening of the second day of the building occupation, Beth's period arrived a week early, leaving her sitting in a pool of rancid red fluid, some of the other students around them whispering and looking sideways. That was the end of their revolutionary stint; Slater had to wrap his jacket around Beth's waist and escort her out of the building, where media people rushed them, wanting to interview them about their defection from the cause. His father had been so pleased to learn that Slater was going to be a part of the student strike that Slater was never able to admit to him that he and Beth had made a premature exit.

Slater drives to downtown Hope Springs to pick up some items for the field trip to Bartlesville. He buys a case of Mountain Dew and a Styrofoam cooler at the Discount Depot, then stops at the pharmacy to pick up some Tylenol and enteric aspirin and a box of Band-Aids. But when he tries to pull open the glass door of the pharmacy, nothing gives. He takes off his shades and reads the sign on the door: *Closed for Memorial Day. See you tomorrow*. Annoyed, Slater heads back to his car, realizing he will need to make a sortie into Walmart. But suddenly he sees something that takes the breath out of him: an old man wearing an American Legion cap, sitting in a lawn chair on the corner, selling paper poppies. Slater feels gut shot, even lurching to one side, off balance. *Poppy*.

Nearly every time he has to reveal to someone the oppressive fact that he lost his father to suicide, the first thing the person says is "How did he do it?" People ask horrible questions, rude and gruesome, and do so with benign, even consoling looks on their faces. Slater has to wonder if he himself might have asked such terrible things, before he became a "suicide survivor." Slater continues to be stunned that rather than offering a politely sympathetic phrase such as "I'm very sorry to hear that,

Dave," they seem to perk up—their voyeurism kicks in immediately. The only thing folks want to know about is the morbid details: did he blow his head off, stab himself in the heart, jump off a bridge, drink drain cleaner? What was that song from the seventies?—"Just blow out your brains, James; jump off the Brooklyn span, Dan; gas yourself in the car, Gar; swallow cyanide, Clyde."

And if asking Slater to furnish the grim details of the means of death is not enough, the next question is inevitably "Did he leave a note?" Why does anyone care, and what does a note have to do with the death of one's father? Is someone's terrible demise supposed to become a source of entertainment?

Fine, cough it up for everyone, he has decided; serve up the ghoulish details on a plate; give them the complete personal horror show. No, there was no note, folks. Poppy's goodbye consisted of messages left on the answering machines of David and his sisters. "Sorry I missed you," Poppy said. "Love ya."

That "Love ya" was the closest his father had ever come in Slater's entire life to saying *I love you, son*. His father had never once said the words "I love you" or even "I'm proud of you," not a single time in Slater's lifetime.

How did he off himself? Slater wishes he could report that his father blew his brains out, a death both dramatic and masculine, a real crowd-pleaser. But no, Poppy never owned a gun, much less shot off his head like Hemingway or even like poor old Hunter Thompson or that kid Cobain. Poppy's death was more like Marilyn Monroe's, an uncharacteristically womanly mode of death. He simply swallowed an entire bottle of barbiturates, crawled between the sheets of his bed as if he were retiring for the night, and expired. The family knew Poppy had been despondent since Mom's death, but they did not learn until after his exit that he had been diagnosed with a malignancy in one lung; Poppy had not chosen to share the bad news with his family. Couldn't he have just had chemo like everyone else?

Beth had been astonished the first time she heard him refer to his father as Poppy. They were still students at the time, only just beginning to become a couple, when in conversation he mentioned Poppy.

"Poppy?" she said, not even bothering to hide her laughter. "Goo-goo Da-Da."

Slater explained that the name Poppy was not a diminutive of Papa but rather referred to the brilliant red flower. Like most men in his age demographic, Poppy had served in World War II. Every year on the eve of Memorial Day—in those days not yet celebrated on Mondays—he came home from the docks wearing a bright paper poppy on his lapel. Slater and his sisters found it hilarious, their father wearing what seemed to them to be a corsage. Mom shushed them, explaining that veterans sold the poppies to raise funds for disabled soldiers, and that Dad was being patriotic. Still, they had begun calling him Poppy after that, and the name stuck.

He pulls his wallet from his back pocket and buys five poppies from the old veteran.

Sorry I missed you.

After waking, Slater lies in bed and halfheartedly considers masturbation, remembering a crudely humorous slogan he once heard: *After fifty, never trust a fart or waste an erection*. Well, he has not yet pooped his pants, but the few spontaneous erections he has now more often than not go to waste. Maybe he has been dreaming about that attractive shrink.

He has not for a fairly long period of time felt himself seriously tempted by an extramarital affair. He and Beth put all that behind them long ago, after some calamitous dalliances in the seventies. In any case, the cheery Baptist women who populate the town are not to his taste. Even if he could stomach them, they wouldn't consider a Jew—he might as well tattoo the mark-o'-the-beast on his forehead. There is no synagogue in the town; he and Beth have to drive an hour and a half to Tulsa during the High Holy Days.

Slater kisses off the possibility of morning onanism and instead gets out of bed. Beth has kicked the blankets and sheet away from her in the night, and her nude body lies motionless on the white bottom sheet like a cadaver on a slab. He cannot help but stare at her thinned-out pubic hair. Where there was once a luxuriant thatch, now there is only the gauziest webbing, her sex revealed like a baby's.

In the bathroom, he decides to change the cartridge in his Quattro and to use some of Beth's aloe moisturizer after he shaves; tonight is the weekly meeting of the grief support group.

Slater observes his hairy chest in the medicine cabinet mirror as he shaves his chin. One cannot ignore the ratio of hair loss to hair growth that is seen on aging bodies. The more hair Slater loses from his head, the more grows on his chest and back, and as for the nose, fuhgeddaboudit—he has had to order one of those trimming devices from the Sharper Image. They say bald men are more virile, so he can perhaps understand the growth of body hair, but what about his ED, as they call it in the pharmaceutical ads. In the three months since Poppy's death, he has been unable to have an erection with Beth. He resorted to ordering Viagra from the Internet, and he and Beth had sex successfully one time about a month ago. The stuff worked great, but it gave him such a blinding headache that he never risked it again. Hell, he read somewhere that even Tommy Lee had tried Viagra, and that the drummer suffered the worst headache of his life.

Beth's sex drive is no longer what it used to be, either, and she too suffers from the inverse hair issue. Though she has barely any pubic hair, he has caught her in the bathroom ripping hair from her upper lip with wax strips, and shaving her toes in the tub. A velvety growth of hair coats her neck, and her formerly pristine thighs now sprout dark hairs. Whoever came up with the expression "aging gracefully" was entirely full of crap.

"Metaphorically at least, he died in my arms," a woman in their circle of metal folding chairs says. She is from Los Angeles. Slater has wondered fairly often why so many of the members of the grief support group are originally from outside Oklahoma. Well, if being devastated by a suicide is what it takes to introduce Slater to some other expats, so be it. He has come to cherish these Wednesday evenings, even though there is bound to be a lot of weeping every week, sometimes his own. The metaphor woman owns a bookstore in Hope Springs, and her fiancé blew his brains out in their bedroom. Slater's chest burns with pain for the poor girl. Those who commit suicide are in fact murderers; Slater has long known this to be true.

The woman herself now addresses this very issue. She tells the group that her little son from an earlier marriage, an eight-year-old boy who had been very fond of his future stepfather, said to his mom, "Reed thought he was killing himself, but really he was killing all his friends." Much nose blowing ensues in the room, and Slater's eyes sting.

Dr. Jane volunteers commentary on the possibility of the woman's son obtaining some counseling, but Slater cannot concentrate on what she is saying. Rather, he finds himself looking again at Jane's bright toenails, pink this time, easily visible in her thong sandals. It's not that he has a foot fetish; rather, he finds looking at her lovely feet quite a bit easier than looking at her uptilted nose or directly into her eyes. Now that he realizes he is hot for her, he feels self-conscious. Slater does not wish her to find his behavior "inappropriate," nor to think of him as some sort of randy bastard, even if that's what he is.

But now Slater feels like a kid in grammar school, because while he has been inattentive, it seems Dr. Jane has steered the conversation elsewhere. "David, what about you?" she says.

Slater feels his ears flame as if he were under a sun lamp. He is embarrassed that he missed the switch in topic. The fact that she called him David instead of Dave heats him up a bit; sometimes using one's proper name instead of a customary nickname seems the more intimate choice. His groin burns hotter than his neck, and for a moment he thinks he feels dizzy.

"Searching," Jane prompts him. "Did you engage in those behaviors?"

He cues right in—just last Wednesday they had been talking about "searching behaviors" in the bereaved. It seems that after one loses a loved one, particularly if the loss is unexpected and sudden, the aggrieved person begins searching for the lost one, walking about the house in a daze, looking under the blankets on the bed, opening closets, and even looking into the bathtub. Equally prevalent is the desire to wear clothing of the deceased. Newly bereaved people are often seen wandering their houses in a fugue state, wearing the lost one's bathrobe or sweater. Sometimes they open the front door and peer out, as if the dead person is simply tardy and any minute will appear on the porch. This all takes place during what Dr. Jane terms the denial phase of grief.

Slater reports that, no, his situation did not mirror the woman's, as his dad was not living with him and Beth at the time of his death and thus Slater had no reason to look for him. Someone else picks up on the conversation and begins to share her experience. But what Slater has not told them is that there was an odd incident, one that frightened Beth. The night after his sister telephoned to tell them about Poppy, Slater walked in his sleep. Beth found him pacing up and down the hall naked at three o'clock in the morning. When she turned on the light, apparently he looked past her with unseeing eyes, and in a voice she later described as "unearthly" he said, "Poppy?" She had to touch his shoulder and tell him several times, "Dave, you're sleepwalking, everything's okay, come back to bed."

He engaged in sleepwalking one other time in his life, when he was four years old. His father went into the hospital for a ruptured appendix—whisked from the house by ambulance attendants and not coming back that evening. The toddler Slater was found by his mother in the middle of the night walking the house in his yellow jammies, making an eerie moaning sound that awakened her. In fact, he can still, more than half a century later, remember his mother picking him up in her arms and carrying him back to bed after he murmured "Daddy?" several times. In the morning, she told him he had been sleepwalking and reminded him that Daddy was in the hospital but would be home very soon. He does not share these recollections with the group; he keeps things to himself, his father's spawn.

What he encountered that night when his mother discovered his nocturnal roaming was a floor made of air, through which he was about to plummet; a cataclysm; the imploding of the universe.

When the university van brings them home from Bartlesville after nine, the students are still talking to one another sotto voce or listening to their iPods, but Slater is wiped out. Field trips are not as invigorating as they used to be when he was a young assistant professor at Pratt. He thinks of all the corny old jokes the borscht-belt comedians used to make about the legs going first. Too bad this turns out to be true—his calves began throbbing while he and the students were still walking Price Tower.

"Did you know that the most common post-disaster injury is cut feet?" one of his students says to her seatmate. Slater is unable to hear the whispered response.

Once the van has pulled into the lot outside the architecture building, Slater makes sure all the students are safely out of the van and into their cars, then climbs into his own car, his knees cracking like adolescent knuckles. God, he feels like he could use a nightcap, but this is a college town and he does not wish to run into any of his students in a bar. He opts to go up instead of down—caffeine rather than alcohol—and stops the car in front of Sancho's.

In his car in the darkened parking lot, Slater's view through the restaurant's enormous plate-glass window is unobstructed. Sancho's blazes in front of his eyes like a brilliant outdoor movie screen, and he feels as if he is back in his childhood, sitting in the backseat of the family car at the Pageant drive-in theater. And it is not Liz Taylor or Pier Angeli who stars in this movie but a more current leading lady: Dr. Jane sits in profile, backlit like an ingénue, sipping from a cup. He recognizes her by her upturned shiksa nose, adorable.

Fatigue renders him loopy. His mind swings from its hinges for a few moments, his thoughts careering into irregular space: I wish for just one day I were not married to Beth. I wish I had hair like Stone Phillips—if he's not wearing a rug, the guy must have had a transplant. I wish I were named Stone instead of Dave. I wish I still lived in New York. I wish I had been a better son. Please, God, let me find a way to get Jane into bed with me and not get caught. God, send Poppy back, if only for a day, an hour.

He watches Jane take a few more sips from the cup. One last thing slides into his mind as it reels along askew, something he once overheard one student say to another as the pair walked across the quad: *You can't pray for what you want. God is not a short-order cook.*

Slater knows he should go home to Beth rather than approach Jane in Sancho's, but he resists the sensible part of his brain, the part that would have him wimp out. I'm going in, he decides—I'm not a eunuch yet. He first takes a whiff of his underarms, just in case the long day in Bartlesville has rendered him rank. He seems to pass muster, so he gets out of the car and approaches Sancho's.

He decides that rather than letting on that he has seen Jane through the window, he should make the encounter seem like a bit of serendipity—he does not want to come off as a stalker. He will casually order a cup of joe and then walk by her table, ostensibly on the way to a seat further in back. If she does not ask him to sit down, he will assert himself, say, Might I join you?

But after he has the coffee in hand and turns away from the counter, something changes. Jane has seen him and is smiling, has even raised one hand slightly in greeting. He wonders how her face looks so young—he is fairly sure she is about his age. Beth posits that Jane has "had some work done" and points out that Jane's hands look much older than her face.

She seems glad to see him. Her teeth are so white, he thinks. He feels himself smile, too, and strides toward her table, but—oh god, this cannot be happening. It's one of those cartoon moments, a scene enacted myriad times in Hollywood comedies, the smile-over-the-shoulder scene, a bit of cheesy slapstick. It seems she is in fact smiling at some guy behind Slater; the smile and the little hand raise are for the other man.

He hears Poppy's voice in his ear: *Tough it out, boy. Never let 'em see you sweat.* He will not let Jane know what has just gone down. He pretends he has only now noticed her and nods in what he hopes is a businesslike manner as he passes her table. Once he is seated, his face engorged with heat, he takes the opportunity to scope out his competition, who is now seated at Jane's table, facing Slater.

It would have been too much to expect that Dr. Jane's companion appear effeminate or perhaps homely or even mildly handicapped. No: the bastard could give Johnny Depp a run for his money. He has dark hair, enough for five men, and wears a tight red T-shirt and Levi's, the red shirt inflaming Slater's ire, the showy son-of-a-bitch. And not only does he appear to be far more handsome and fit than Slater, he also appears to be tremendously younger; the guy looks barely thirty. For one goofy moment, he thinks maybe the guy's her son.

But no, Jane and sonny-boy are doing what the entertainment programs on TV call "canoodling," nothing flagrant, but a lot of looking into each other's eyes and a bit of fingertip touching.

What was I thinking? he wonders. I'm done, the guy with the Doberman had it right when he called me "old-timer." My parents are dead and I'm flat-out next in line for the Slater family plot. And there will be no one behind me in that grim queue. Maybe we should have had kids; at least some of my DNA would remain in the universe. No wonder I can't get it up: I'm kaput.

In the car on the way home, Slater attempts to tamp down his distress by turning up the volume on the radio, the Oklahoma City NPR station. The first thing he hears is the interviewer asking someone described as a scientist/professor, "So, are you saying that the invisibility cloak may no longer be simply science fiction?"

The man answers, "Yes, you could actually make someone invisible as long as he wears a cloak made of this material." It seems the guy is in the process of creating a cloak made of what is termed metamaterials, which can be tuned to bend electromagnetic radiation and visible light in any direction. The scientist claims, "We think we can present a solid case for making invisibility an attainable goal."

When Slater was nine years old, one of his uncles gave him a radio-controlled whoopee cushion for his birthday. The thing looked like a typical accent pillow and could be strategically placed for the chosen mark to sit on. The young Slater could control the device from another location, causing deplorable honks of flatulence to issue from the unsuspecting sitter's behind. The first time he tried out the device on his parents and sisters, everyone in the room laughed when he cried out, "It's a dream come true!" But the real dream-come-true would be an invisibility cloak. Since early childhood he has had a persistent fantasy of walking the earth in a mantle of invisibility.

The wind has picked up, and as Slater drives home he can see that it's about to rain. A loud, sharp crack of thunder causes him to flinch. But the thunder booming above him also initiates kinesis of his mind. He finds himself transported back to the first time he can recall hearing thunder, before he even knew what it was. He was at the time about the same age he was when his father had the appendectomy and had felt not exactly frightened but surprised when he heard a peal of thunder above the family home, as if a convoy of trucks was driving across the roof. His father explained to him then about thunder and lightning and took him to the window to observe the lightning flashes. He told his son that soon rain would begin to fall.

When Slater asked how his father knew this, Poppy told him that rain inevitably followed thunder and lightning. "When it starts to rain, can I go outside?" he asked Poppy.

His father said as long as he cleared it with Mom, that would be fine. His mother dressed Slater in a slicker, red rubber boots, and a sou'wester rain hat, and he stood at the window until he saw the rain begin to fall. Poppy joined him then, wearing a Giants sweatshirt and a hard hat. He held young Slater's hand in his callused paw and led him out into the garden. They sat on deck chairs near the lilacs and honeysuckle, faces upturned, Davey Slater opening his mouth to catch the raindrops.

In the driveway in front of his house, Slater sits in the car in the rain, staring at the porch light that Beth has switched on, feeling immobile and heavy as if his body is a sack of meal. His heart breaks for a moment when he spots that poor wasp still circling on the porch, slow to get the point that he is now homeless.

He sits at first inert in the car, but before he knows it, his notebook is out and he is making a list beneath the glare of the dome light:

THINGS TO DO IN THE INVISIBILITY CLOAK:

1. *God forgive me, but: follow Dr. Jane home and get the goods on her— is red shirt her lover? Does she look as good naked as she does with her clothes on?*

2. *Wear the cloak to the grief support group and listen to what they say about me when they think I'm not there.*

3. *Follow Beth—see if she has an alternate life. Does she have some man with billows of hair, who never smells like garlic?*

4. *For this one, need time machine as well as invisibility cloak: Let me be with Poppy when he dies. If I cannot change what happened, at least let me be there to prevent my father from dying alone.*

Slater stops writing, then rips the page from the notebook and crumples it. He does not wish anyone ever to learn of his base wishes and pitiful regrets—let him put an invisibility cloak around those.

He thinks of Dracula. Dracula wore a cloak. And Superman, though his was more of a cape. If Slater wore a Superman cape, he could fly through the sky with his arms out in front of him like the young, unmaimed Chris Reeve, perhaps carrying a Lois Lane (or a Dr. Jane) in his arms, a hero. Or he could don a darker cape, the Dracula stealth cape, which he could wrap around his creamy prey before he sank his teeth into her lovely stem of a neck and took them both all the way, all the way to eternal life.

Suddenly Beth appears in the driveway and raps her knuckles on the driver's side window. When he rolls down the window, Slater sees his wife is weeping, her nose streaming and eyes red. He looks at her, at first uncomprehending. But then he realizes, my poor Beth, she knows the man she married might now as well be a thousand miles into the stratosphere.

"Come inside, Dave," she says. "You've been sitting here for half an hour." The rain has become a soaking downfall, and Beth's hair hangs in wet sheaves, lightning illuminating her face like a flashbulb shot capturing a catastrophe. "It's just the grief," Beth says, "the grief, that's all it is."

He leans out the car window, reaching toward Beth, the cold rain soaking his outstretched hand. His wife's weeping has a muffled quality, as if she cries behind a partition. She seems far away, pearly in the downpour like a Las Vegas stage illusion.

What is vivid in this moment is Slater's vision of what might be possible. He sees himself now, flying back to the scene of that dismal afternoon, this time wearing his invisibility cloak. He swoops down on the casket before the ghoulish undertakers can lower his father into the soil.

THE SUICIDE CLUB

If you would have a thing shrink,
You must first stretch it.

Tao Te Ching

Holly learned the Vicks VapoRub trick from a long-ago boyfriend, a fire-fighter. When firefighters need to perform cadaver removal from an accident site, they goop up their upper lips with the ointment, as it does a fine job of masking the odor of decomposing corpses. She stands in front of the bathroom medicine cabinet, rubbing a thick glob of VapoRub underneath her nose. The burn of the menthol fumes rising in her nostrils furnishes blessed relief, even if the smell clashes with the sandalwood incense she has lit. Until she remembered the factoid about Vicks, she had not been sleeping well, because of the stench.

Her cadavers are those of rodents, poisoned mice that died in the crawl space beneath her house. Friends warned her not to put poison in the basement, that the vermin would die on her property and smell up the house, but what else could she do? She was not about to set out traps and then be faced with the pungent remains of squashed mice. One needs a husband to dispose of trapped rodents. Or a fiancé, but Reed is as dead as the mice.

After she slips into bed, she remembers that she has not yet checked the Web for today's prospects. Does she care enough to get up and log on, or should she let the search wait until morning? She thinks she hears a rustling—is it Teddy; is he okay? But then she remembers her eight-year-old son is in California with his dad for the summer. Oh gosh, what if the sound is a mouse? She is sitting up now, not having really intended to, just like stories she has heard about dead bodies flipping up into a sitting position in a particularly vigorous case of rigor mortis.

She listens awhile, hears nothing. She beams a flashlight around the room and into the closet, sees nothing. Now she is hyper-alert. She may as well go online.

Her group therapist, Dr. Jane, suggested the online dating service, an idea that at first mortified Holly. Never in her life did she imagine that she would have to troll for dates; she has never been hard up for men. Until now. And though she would never say this to anyone, she has always felt that matchmaking, like Broadway musicals, is something more in the purview of Jewish folks than of WASPs. But, as Dr. Jane told the members of the suicide survivors group Holly attends, one needs to be proactive if one expects to move into the final stage of grief. One needs to integrate the loss and move on.

Holly brings her laptop into bed and logs on to e-Luv. She has chosen as her screen name Sandy_Agow, a subliminal nod to her birthplace, San Diego. The first two weeks she was a member of e-Luv, she was thrilled every morning to check for potential dates, hoping that just the right man would pop up on the screen, a man who could make her let go of Reed—"integrate" the loss. But the progression of men has included a long queue of undesirables. She has been sent men with no hair, men with poor grammar, men named Les and Ralph and Wally, men who have personal relationships with Jesus, men who read Ayn Rand, men who bowl.

Tonight Divorcé #1 at first looks like an actual possibility: he has thick dark hair, intense brown eyes, and at first glance nothing seems wrong with him. But as she reads his profile, disappointment washes over her. He is named Sandor, and he reveals he has never been married (at age forty-nine). In the space where one is asked to reply to "What secret about you do only your best friends know?" he states that he cries very easily. She zooms on his posted photo to increase its size, and she now sees that the poor man has a weak chin. Sure, answering a question like that can be tough; her own answer was "Find out, Mister!"

The boxes to check to indicate religion include Christian, Jewish, spiritual but not affiliated with any particular religion, atheist, and other. He has checked "other." What is he, a male Wiccan? No, those people are usually tremendously obese. Maybe he's a full-bore Satanist, a weeping Satanist.

E-Luv enables its clients to click on a box that says, "Close match now." She clicks this box at the bottom of weepy Sandor's page. His face vaporizes into cyberspace.

The odor of sandalwood is beginning to ease her into a better frame of mind. She has lit incense in every room in the house, and sandalwood-ginger scented-oil candles burn in the bedroom, and the fragrance has broken through the VapoRub. Maybe the aromatherapy concept is not hokum, after all.

Divorcé #2 is named Cliff. He would not be so bad if he had known enough to shave off the mustache that gives him that seventies look. But she cannot really post on the e-Luv Contact Board a message advising Cliff that he needs to lose the mustache if he expects to get a woman. She does not wish to sound as shallow as some of the men on e-Luv do. One of them, a very handsome guy with a full head of hair and a cleft chin, specified exactly what kind of woman he wanted: "A wholesome, Monica Potter type," he stated. He had added, just in case, "Look her up." Holly had, against her better judgment, googled Monica Potter. She learned the woman was a young blond actress. Potter's shoulder-length hair blew in the wind in one of the photos on the Web. From the looks of her, she was probably twenty years younger than the bachelor. Holly remembered a Randy Newman song from when she was a kid, in which Newman sang, "Jesus, what a jerk."

Holly is happy to be at work; the shop smells like books. Sometimes she thinks the real reason she decided to open a bookstore was so she could breathe in the scent of books all day, six days a week—the ink, the paper, the cloth of the hardbounds—as heady as an aphrodisiac. *H. Hemenway, Booksellers*, reads the sign on the shop's facade. The "s" forming the plural "booksellers" represents a bit of a pose, as she is sole owner and the only real salesperson, unless you count Cadon, the college student she employs part-time, who is a desultory salesperson at best. Using what was left of her divorce settlement to pull up stakes in Los Angeles and open her own bookstore in a college town in Oklahoma was a very bad choice in today's business climate, with independent bookstores falling like dominos. And the fact is, she had never so much as taken a business course in college, nor had she ever worked as a shopgirl when she was still a student. Her job history consists of only two places of employment: an editorial position at Houghton Mifflin after she graduated and a tech writing job in L.A. with the Motion Picture Academy's film archives.

Reed had been given a great opportunity with a start-up in Oklahoma City, or so he claimed. Holly had been so crazy about him that she could not bear to stay behind in California when he decided to move to OKC. The past few months have made it clear that one might be advised not to buy a bookstore just because one likes to read and has worked in the publishing end of the book business. She has begun to realize that she may be like the fat guy who loves to eat and to cook but who goes belly-up when he opens a restaurant.

The shop is empty this morning, save for her and Cadon. She has opened up only moments before and is rearranging some greeting cards on a rack before the walk-in traffic begins. The bar mitzvah cards are not selling and are beginning to look dusty and faded—she should have known not to order ethnic or non-Christian cards in a place like Hope Springs. She assumed the state university campus in town would include a sufficient number of Jewish faculty, but apparently either she guessed incorrectly or the Jewish faculty are keeping a very low profile in Hope Springs. The Christian bookstore a few blocks away from Hemenway's does a thriving business in didactic tomes, "inspirational" fiction, the *Left Behind* series, and greeting cards that feature images of angels or of Jesus.

Cadon has put on a Sade CD, which hits just the right note today. She wonders how Cadon even knows about Sade—her fame was before his time. The twenty-somethings of today—the Cadons and Jadons and Aidens and Braedens—are not likely to know who Sade is. Holly has found that, often as not, young adults are ignorant of Bhopal, do not know who Gorbachev was, and have never heard of *The Satanic Verses*. And as for the old black-and-white Hollywood films she learned to love when she was working at the Academy archives: not a chance. The younger generation wants action films, movies with computer-generated images like that *Silver Surfer* thing.

She is of the Matt and Steve and Jeff generation, those who listened not only to Guns N' Roses but also to Sade. *Is it a crime?* Oh dear, the CD playing reminds her of a weekend on Padre Island with Reed—the little bistro in the hotel played a lot of Sade. Don't think about sex, she tells herself. The bell over the door tinkles and she looks up.

The man who enters the shop is Dave, an older guy from Dr. Jane's suicide survival group. He's from New York, and Holly found him brassy, even abrasive, until she began to know him better.

Dave approaches the card rack where she stands. "Interesting that you would name a bookstore Hemingway's," he says.

She has become accustomed to the fact that Dave seldom offers salutations or greetings, just jumps into conversation in medias res.

"Good morning, Dave," she says. "Actually, it's Hemenway's, not Hemingway's—Hemenway is my last name."

He expels a short laugh. "Funny, I never knew your last name. I guess the Suicide Club is like A.A.—we're all supposed to be anonymous."

For a moment Holly draws a blank. Oh my gosh, he calls the grief support group the Suicide Club? She is not sure if he is being cynical or just making an offbeat joke, so she wills her expression to remain impassive.

"Do you have the last Chris Hitchens book?" he says.

"You mean *God Is Not Great?*" she says, keeping her voice fairly low. A couple has just come in, and they are more likely to be looking for *The Purpose Driven Life* than the Hitchens. As the man and woman come closer, Holly hopes they did not hear her say, "God is not great." She goes to the back of the store and fetches the Hitchens for Dave, who has followed her to the shelves. She hands him the volume, asking if he needs anything further.

"This ought to do it," he says. "My wife and I saw someone last night on the Hair Network railing against this book," Dave adds. "We figure if they hate it, we'll love it."

"The Hair Network?" Dave always makes her feel slow, the way most New Yorkers do. What is the Hair Network, she wonders—something like the Hair Club for Men? Dave does have a significant bald spot.

"You know," Dave says. "One of those Trinity Broadcasting stations—the ones where they preach the ol' fire-and-brimstone and all the televangelists wear pompadours," he says. "Lot of black hair dye."

She cannot help but smile, then turns to wait on the couple, directing Dave to Cadon at the register.

"Going tomorrow night?" Dave says.

The Suicide Club. Yes, she is.

As she drives home from the shop, Holly decides about dinner. She will have what she thinks of as "the modified Atkins"—a porterhouse accompanied by half a bottle of Cabernet. She wishes Teddy would be home to have dinner with her, but, per the joint custody agreement, he is in L.A. with her ex until school starts in the fall. During the year since Reed killed himself, Holly has grown increasingly anxious over custody transfers. Theo now questions her suitability as a parent. Although Teddy was not in the house at the time Reed pulled the trigger, the suicide has made the premises, in Theo's eyes, a charnel house—far too unsavory an environment for his little boy. When her ex learned of Reed's suicide, all he said was "It was always clear to me the son-of-a-bitch was no gentleman." She did not point out to Theo that some of his own consorts have not exactly been cotillion material.

She sneezes sharply and her eyes involuntarily close; the car swerves out of its lane. As she sneezes again, she nearly sideswipes a car with a bumper sticker saying, "A dusty Bible means a dirty life." She spent some time this afternoon in the stockroom at the shop and is likely sneezing from that particular dust.

Holly has to wonder if Theo might not be correct—maybe Reed's death has warped Teddy in some way, especially since Reed and her son were buddies from the get-go. She should check into whether there is a suicide survivors group in Hope Springs for children but figures she instead might need to take him to a child psychologist in Tulsa. She has not told Theo about this, but this spring when she took their son to see the film *Bambi*, Teddy was the only person in the theater—child or adult—who did not shed a tear when Bambi's mother died. Holly was shaken by his stoicism, which seemed unnatural. But was it the death of a mother that failed to move her child, or was he showing signs of emotional blunting due to the trauma of Reed's death? She hardly knows which is worse.

Maybe having a whole bottle of wine on hand for tonight might be advisable, she figures—the modified-modified Atkins. But thanks to the nutty blue laws in Oklahoma, she will not be able to pick up a bottle of wine at the grocery store when she buys the porterhouse. She sneezes again, then turns left at the Christian bookstore, parks the car in front of the tribal tobacco outlet, and walks over to the liquor store.

When Holly arrives at Bethel Baptist, where Dr. Jane McAllister holds the Wednesday night suicide-survivors workshop, she sees that she is the last person to arrive and that Dave is already talking. She missed last week's session, as the sneezing fit after work turned out to be the first sign of a brutal cold. Dr. Jane wears a pale yellow linen suit and is nodding at whatever Dave has just said, and she gives a wink of acknowledgment as Holly enters the room.

"And then my sister was on my case like stank on a monkey," Dave says.

SueAnn, a forty-something lady whose teenage son killed himself, offers a few examples of her own tussles with relatives after her son's death, and Dr. Jane reminds everyone that in the wake of tragedy, often the worst comes out in people, and that this is understandable. When the room goes silent, Holly apologizes for being late, and for missing last week's session.

Dr. Jane inquires, "Are you okay now?"

"My cold's gone," Holly says. But she hears her voice crack on the word "gone," and to her embarrassment, tears form and cling to her lower lashes.

"Is there something wrong, Holly?" Dr. Jane says.

Can she really tell them what has upset her? Almost certainly they will find her narcissistic, and what is bothering her is hardly grief.

"I went to the urgent-care clinic to get some medicine for my sore throat," she says. "And to make sure I didn't have bronchitis." She pauses and watches everyone look inquisitively at her. "The doctor, a man, when he took my history asked me if I were still menstruating."

"And your age is only . . . ?" SueAnn says.

"Thirty-six." She instantly feels as if she has Tourette's, impulsively blurting out, "The dumb bastard."

"Perhaps that wasn't very judicious of him," Dr. Jane says. "When I was in grad school, we were taught never to ask that question—even if the patient were in her seventies. We were told to ask, 'When was your last period?'"

"I don't get it," Dave says, looking genuinely puzzled.

SueAnn says, "Holly don't look old enough for menopause. And no gal likes being thought of as a dried-up ol' thing—sure she's upset!"

Holly feels shamed, not only because the doctor assumed she was old, but also because her reproductive functions are being discussed in a group setting. She uses a longtime coping device, a little internal mantra that she taught herself in elementary school: I'm-not-here-now, I'm-not-here-now, I, am, not, here, now. She focuses intently on Dr. Jane's shoes, channeling all her energy into studying them, homing in on the visual and tuning out the aural. Dr. Jane always looks as if she is dressed for Major Metropolitan, not Hope Springs, Oklahoma. Holly has never seen her wear jeans or polyester blouses or matronly shoes. She suspects Dr. Jane would not ever be caught wearing Birkenstocks as Holly does to-night. Jane is wearing bone T-straps with a three-inch heel and acutely pointed toes.

Only this morning, Holly noticed a Dillard's shoe-sale advertise-ment in the newspaper and found herself lingering over the ad. The shoes pictured all had women's names assigned to the respective styles: high-heeled mules named Rochelle, sandals named Jill, wedges named Norma. Who decided to give shoes women's names? she wonders. She considers whether a shoe called Holly would be a Birki or a stiletto or a loafer.

She brings herself back into the room and sees that Dave is again speaking. "Yeah, my wife slapped me in the face once when I told her she was acting menopausal."

Holly arrives home from the shop, carrying groceries into the kitchen. She and Reed bought the house only six months before his death, and though she can no longer sleep in the bedroom that was hers and Reed's, she does not wish to sell the house.

She and Teddy and Reed's Irish setter, Joyce, stayed with her mother in the immediate aftermath, and a few days later, when the yellow police tape came down and Holly began to regain some of her equilibrium, she numbly thumbed through the classifieds until she found the heading Crime Scene Restoration. The ad that caught her attention was the one that contained, in large block letters, the promise LIKE IT NEVER HAPPENED!

When she came home from work that terrible day, she had called out the ironic "Honey, I'm home!" that was Reed's and her habitual greeting, but there was no response, except that Joyce jumped up on her as he always did when Holly came home. "Down, Joyce. Reed?" she called. Nothing. Not seeing Reed in the kitchen or the study where he usually worked, she climbed the stairs to the bedroom.

She now knows that most often it is men who shoot themselves. Statistics indicate that women rarely choose a gunshot to the head as their mode of suicide. There is conjecture that most women find the idea of mutilating their faces the most undesirable way to go. Women usually swallow pills, or sometimes sit in their cars and breathe in carbon monoxide. Holly had always imagined, though, that one tiny gunshot to the temple would not be all that bad and certainly would be quicker than taking pills and having to lie down and wait to die. She had imagined a tiny, bullet-sized indentation in the temple, bleeding slightly at the entrance site, and envisioned perhaps a slightly larger exit wound somewhere else in the head. Neat, practical, effective. It was not as if one needed to ram a shotgun into her mouth and blow off her face. No, what Nancy Reagan had once termed "a tiny little gun" placed strategically at one temple did not seem too grotesque.

But when she entered the bedroom, though it took several moments for what she was seeing to actually seem real, all she could think of in her dumb horror was photos she had seen of Jackie Kennedy in a pink suit splattered gruesomely with crimson-brown blood. Reed lay on the floor, his face obscured by gore, an evil scarlet halo on the carpet beneath his head. The amount of blood on the walls and ceiling shocked Holly to the core.

She wishes she could say that she had run to Reed, stooped to take his pulse or to perform CPR, or even knelt to pray. But the fact is, she did exactly what that sixties comedian Lenny Bruce claimed Mrs. Kennedy did when her husband was shot: "hauled ass."

To be accurate, Holly *crawled* ass. She sank to her knees as if she were a plastic blow-up doll with a slow leak, a slow descent to the formerly eggshell carpet. She scooted along on her belly down the hall to the phone, crawling like a blindworm with Joyce creeping along with her, whimpering.

The crime-scene-restoration company had done wonders with the bedroom. After they were finished, Holly could find no trace of the blood that had punctuated the room. The workers asked her permission to discard the black-and-white movie posters that dressed up the walls. Fred and Ginger and Clark and Claudette were blood spattered, which morbidly called to mind the old riddle from elementary school: What's black and white and red all over? She did not even see the gun until after the police arrived—a 12-gauge shotgun. The fact that Reed owned a shotgun came as a total surprise to her. She cannot imagine where he must have been hiding the thing.

What used to be the bedroom is now the guest room and vice versa. Though the former guest room is smaller than Holly and Reed's bedroom, it does not feel as spooked. But of course Reed is still dead, and she is now a bombed-out hull and thus a member of the Suicide Club. As with the crime-scene-fixing company, she found Dr. Jane's grief support group in the Yellow Pages, in this case online.

Her laptop sits on the kitchen table where she left it this morning. She logs on to e-Luv. A man has e-mailed her: "Damn your cute Sandy." She immediately zaps him, then clicks on the profile of a decent-looking bearded man named Larry. As she reads his profile, nothing about him strikes her one way or the other; he seems fairly generic. But as Holly reads over Larry's responses to the list of e-Luv-provided questions, she is stopped short by one of these. The question is "Name four things you cannot live without." When perusing some of the past male responses, she has noticed that the answers seem to run the gamut from "my boat" to "my kids" to "good wine" to "excitement" to inappropriate statements about sex. But poor Larry has answered "air, water, food, sleep." She looks back to the top of the page and sees that he has listed his occupation as civil engineer.

But her late fiancé, Reed, had plenty of imagination, along with good looks, bedroom skills, intelligence, and wit. Only fly in that VapoRub was that he also shot himself in their bedroom; probably Larry would not do such a thing.

She snaps shut the computer's lid, opens the bottle of Cabernet, and pours herself a glass. When Joyce nuzzles her, begging, she dips her finger into the glass and lets the dog lick off the wine. Holly lowers her face to Joyce's furry head, breathes in the familiar musky smell. That was the worst thing in the days following Reed's death: she could smell his hair everywhere she went, as if the scent clung to the inside of her nose like a fragrant mist. Her hands, too, had tingled, nearly vibrated, with the phantom pain of feeling Reed's curly hair. She sits at the kitchen table, staring at nothing. Her hips, seeming heavy as a sandbag, moor her to the chair. The dead-mouse smell creeps up through the floorboards, eradicating any yearnings for dinner. She should get up and light some candles and incense. Maybe she ought to call back the restoration company and see if they can find the bodies and haul them out. *I'm not here now, I'm not here.*

"I'm alive in the moment, present here and now," Holly recites, then repeats the affirmation several times. She is sitting in a chair across from Dr. Jane in the psychologist's office on the university campus. Holly has scheduled a private session, having begun to feel mildly alienated by the group meetings. Her usual mantra is deemed by Jane a "dissociative reaction" and something of which she should divest herself. Jane herself has suggested the replacement mantra "I'm alive in the moment, present here and now." Holly feels like a talking computer, as she does not for a moment feel alive in the moment, present here and now. If she wanted to sabotage the session, all she would need to do is voice for Dr. Jane the as yet unspoken mantra, the one that comes closest to the truth: *I'm dead every moment, world without end, amen.*

Instead Holly says, "Reed might still be alive if it weren't for me. It's all my fault." She cannot forget what he left as a suicide note: *Goodbye, cruel world!* He even remembered the comma between "goodbye" and "cruel." She did not know then, nor does she now, whether the message demonstrated mordant humor or whether Reed actually meant *Goodbye, cruel Holly.*

She conjectures again that Reed's gambling might not have escalated so ferociously if they had stayed in L.A. The combination of being cut off from his friends and family and spending too much time online had driven Reed deep into Internet poker and then Indian gambling casinos—"gaming" casinos as they are euphemistically phrased. He had slid right off the edge and gone down quickly. She does not need to tell Dr. Jane about the quarrel the night before Reed died.

"What about the money he stole from you, though?" Jane says.

"He took it, more than stole it," Holly says.

Jane says, "Where's your rage? Are you intent on making a saint out of him just because he's dead?"

I don't have any rage, Holly thinks but says nothing. Poor Reed—how can she rage against someone desperate enough to take his own life?

It has begun suddenly to rain. Holly is still not accustomed to the summer storms in Oklahoma, which come quickly out of nowhere and rumble overhead like the Heartland Flyer train. The rainwater pounds the windows and skylight in Dr. Jane's office, and Holly mercifully cannot hear what Jane is saying. She sits inert, watching Jane's lips move like an actor's on TV when the sound is turned off. In the weeks before Reed's death, he often sat in front of the TV smoking Camels and staring at the screen with the sound muted. When Holly entered the room, he would turn to her with the look of dull glass in his eyes. The rain escalates as Dr. Jane's lips offer subaudible counsel.

———

As Holly walks across campus from Dr. Jane's office to the lot where she parked her car, the sun bearing down on the back of her neck makes her feel like a burger under a broiler. She has left Cadon in charge of the shop, so when she spots an on-campus café called Kampus Koffee she decides to stop for an iced tea. She pulls open the glass door and immediately spots Dave from the suicide survivors group. Her impulse is to push the door closed and go elsewhere.

But Dave has seen her. She gives him a small wave, and he stands and makes a "sit here" gesture, pointing to the chair across from him. Holly complies as Dave nudges aside the spiral notebook he was writing in.

Once Holly has ordered and she and Dave exchange a few pleasantries, silence sets in and she feels as if she should get the conversational ball in the air. She knows he is a professor of architecture at the university, so she says the first thing that comes to mind, "Sketching out a building?" and points to the notebook near his cup. She instantly regrets the moronic inquiry, but heck, is she expected to begin a dialogue about Buckminster Fuller or something?

Dave comes as close to looking flustered as she has ever seen him. His hand moves to shield what he has written, and color rises in his face. "It's just a list," he tells her. "Sometimes when I'm idle I make lists—it's nothing, really."

"Let me see," she says.

Just as Holly complied when he indicated she sit with him, Dave passively hands over the notebook. "Things That Look Like Other Things" is the scrawled heading. She reads the list:

1: *Men named Buck or Rowdy who look like accountants*

2: *Women named Joy who might better have been named Dolores, or even Oleander*

3: *Zucchini, which look like cucumbers*

4: *Penguins*

My gosh, what a strange little man he is, Holly thinks. Before she looks up from the list, she attempts to keep her face deadpan. "I don't understand about the penguins," she says.

Dave says, "Did you see that movie about the marching penguins?"

When Holly nods, Dave continues, still appearing a bit embarrassed. "The film depressed the hell out of me," he says. "The damn birds do nothing but suffer from birth to death. Even the act of conception seems grim."

Not knowing what to say, Holly only shrugs.

"I'm a Jew, you know," Dave says, "but in school I studied Eastern religions, and something from the *Tibetan Book of the Dead* always stuck with me."

Holly nods again, waiting.

"I'm not saying I believe this," Dave says, "but the *Book of the Dead* says that if you wreck your karma, you get stuck on the karmic wheel and are likely to be reincarnated—transmigrated they call it—as an animal. I don't want to be a fuckin' penguin."

Holly is nonplussed. Dave has heretofore seemed like a fairly pragmatic guy. "And you feel as if you've damaged your karma?" she says.

The volume of Dave's voice decreases to just above a whisper. "I wasn't there for my dad."

She reminds Dave that Dr. Jane says all suicide survivors feel guilty.

"Maybe so, but Poppy had cancer and I was so self-involved I didn't even know it. Truth be told, I hadn't even called him in half a year." Dave looks so aggrieved that Holly feels compelled to share her own guilt.

"I can top that," she says. "The night before Reed shot himself, he said to me in a really quiet voice, 'I'm no good.' You know what I said to him?"

Dave shakes his head.

"I said, 'Darling, I've been telling you that for months!'"

They hold each other's gaze, words unnecessary. Only a suicide survivor really knows another; that much Holly has learned. Dave reaches across the small round table and places his hand paternally over hers, patting her as if she were an infant. Dave's face across the table is mournful and kind. From the crown of her head, Holly feels an inchoate glow of warm radiance, luminance. The feeling disperses through her body, as if she were being filled like a balloon and might rise up from the wrought-iron chair and hover at the ceiling like the floating Little Mermaid in the Macy's parade.

Dave offers to walk Holly to her car, but she declines and trudges back to the lot where she parked the Mustang. She has not told anyone other than Dave, not even Dr. Jane, about the terrible thing she said to Reed the night before he committed suicide. She cannot fathom what made her cough it up to Dave. Maybe she saw evidence in his stricken countenance that he too carried a corpse on his back. His transgression seems to Holly so much less malignant then her own. *He hadn't phoned his father in months*—in her view, no huge malfeasance. She, however, had answered Reed as if she were Nora Charles tossing off a sassy line of dialogue in a 1930s *Thin Man* movie.

But she was no Myrna Loy, no glamour-girl comedic leading lady. She was the person who hauled ass, leaving her beloved face up in a pool of congealing blood. Dave's point about karma has hit home with her, and she knows she would be getting off easy if she came back as a penguin.

Teddy telephones just after Holly finishes dinner. He and his father went to the beach today, Teddy says, and he is still giddy with the thrill of sand, breaking waves, and Sno-Cones. Theo took Teddy to Santa Monica Pier, and Teddy is effusive about riding the bumper cars. She asks to speak to Daddy, ready to ask Theo if she can have Teddy back a couple of weeks early.

In response to her query, Theo says, "What the hell would he do there—go to Jesus camp?"

"There are other activities," she says, knowing that Theo is correct: summer for children in Hope Springs consists of Vacation Bible Camp, and even the woods are beset by deer flies and chiggers. Holly caves more easily than she would normally, not wishing to be overly selfish. She cannot deprive Teddy of California beaches and subject him to a parched summer in a landlocked state so backward it does not even have a major league baseball team. "We'll stick to what we planned," she says, then speaks briefly again to Teddy before she hangs up.

She is still somewhat unsettled by her session with Dr. Jane, and by the odd interlude with Dave in the café. She roots in a kitchen drawer for matches so she can spark up some calming candles and incense, but as she lights a white lotus candle, she realizes that the mouse cadaver smell has notably abated. Maybe the downpour of rain somehow purged the odor from the basement and purified the air. Or maybe the smell at last simply dissipated. By the time Teddy comes home, the house will probably smell fine.

She has brought home from the shop a copy of the *Tao Te Ching*, recommended by Dave, which she sets down on the table and will begin reading while she eats dinner. Dave claims the book helps him deal with the loss of his father. But before Holly starts dinner, she checks e-Luv. The matches she has been sent today are all either ugly as gargoyles or Pentecostal or Republican. She dispenses with the "matches" and scrolls through photos of non-matches, looking for someone appealing. When she gets to page 10, like a "Yes!" floating up in the fluid in a Magic 8-Ball, a photo of a man closely resembling Reed becomes visible. For one exquisite, awful moment, she thinks the man actually is Reed—that the promise has been magically fulfilled, *like it never happened*.

Waiting4U is the man's screen name, allowing Holly to continue to think of him as Reed. The most unlikely thing is that the man's hair is the same shade as Reed's: dark red, not the carrot-top red one most often sees, but a rare deep burnt carmine. Like Reed, the man has black eyebrows and slightly swarthy skin. What is even more improbable is the sole dimple on one side of his mouth, exactly like Reed's. She indulges in a momentary fantasy, the sort of unlikely scenario one encounters in soap operas: Reed has a twin they never knew about, and she has now found him. She knows such things can actually happen. Only a few months ago she read in the *Tulsa World* that in Ecuador a chance meeting had reunited twin sisters who never knew of the other's existence.

Holly sees that Waiting states the last "good book" he read was (but of course!) *The Purpose Driven Life*. She thinks of Dave's list from earlier today—things that look like other things—and is reminded of Lauren Bacall. The actress once married Jason Robards, and the consensus was that she did so only because the actor resembled Humphrey Bogart. Bogie had been the love of Bacall's life; evidently, when she saw Robards, she felt that through some sort of necromancy she could again be made love to by Bogart. The marriage had not worked out.

Now Holly sees that Waiting is not a divorced man but a widower. She scrutinizes the rest of his profile, scrolling doggedly up and down, looking for signs of Reed-kinship. Waiting was born in Texas, where he still resides, whereas Reed was born in Colorado. That does not mean they might not still be twins, though—if Waiting was adopted out, his actual place of birth might have been "revised." But he claims to be thirty-five and a Taurus, whereas Reed was thirty-eight and a Pisces.

Under "Favorite Things to Do" Waiting has written: "Watch sports on my widescreen, ride my Harley, watch movies (favorite: all James Bond), dance at C&W clubs, and especially—cheer on the Cowboys. But none of those since my wife passed away. I don't really have any favorite things to do, anymore. Maybe I signed up for e-Luv too soon, sorry."

Holly's guts whirlpool, and she feels sweat bead on her upper lip. Grief trumps country-and-western bars, even trumps that awful book. She sits staring at the pulsing cursor on the screen, her hands motionless on the keyboard, but Joyce begins to whine to go outside. She writes: "Dear Waiting4U, I lost someone, too." She sits a few moments more, then impulsively reaches across the table for the *Tao Te Ching*. She has always believed that a book can help just about anything. She opens randomly to a page and chooses what she will send to Waiting4U:

> *A man is supple and weak when living, but petrified and*
> *   immutable when dead.*
> *Grass and trees are fragile and pliant when living, but dried and*
> *   shriveled when dead.*
> *Thus, the steely and the strong are the comrades of death;*
> *The supple and the weak are the comrades of life.*

She types the verses carefully, then adds "(from Lao Tzu)" and "If you feel like e-mailing me, my real name is Holly."

Before she can change her mind, she clicks Send. Something surges inside her. Who ever knows what might happen, anyway? With a roll of the dice, the universe can transmute. Faster than a speeding bullet.

She flings open the kitchen's French doors to let the dog outside and Joyce vaults out to the yard. Inhaling deeply, Holly smells the rain-washed air. The Oklahoma red-clay soil seems to glow in the dusk like smoldering coals. In the distance stands a water tower, the painted-on words visible from her yard: Hope Springs. She stands motionless at the threshold, thinking she hears something. Can it be someone whispering, something slithering? She sees nothing out of the ordinary, so she listens intently. There is a barely perceptible buzzing sibilance, and Holly senses an invisible presence. Beyond her is the known world, the mountainless vastness of the plains.

BELVEDERE

For I am poor and needy,
and my heart is wounded within me.

Psalms 100:22

SueAnn's jaw pops out of its socket, and she cries out, "Oh! Ma'am, please." The pain is concentrated and intense, as if a laser is cutting into her jawbone.

The mammography technician barely takes notice of her, other than to ask disinterestedly, "Are we compressing your breast too much?" She continues to squash SueAnn's breast against a cold metal plate.

SueAnn pulls back from the apparatus. "It's not that," she mumbles. She draws a deep breath, thunks herself on the left side of her face, then cradles her chin in her two hands. "You'll have to excuse me, ma'am. My jaw—it snapped out of joint when you pulled down on my shoulder."

The technician says nothing, and SueAnn realizes the woman does not believe that the shoulder manipulation was the cause of the jaw slip—a "TMJ issue," as her dentist terms the jaw problem.

"Ahh, that's better. Back where it belongs," SueAnn says.

"Are you ready now?" the woman says, her voice overly pleasant and artificially nurturing in the way that really means go to heck.

She says she is fine, and the technician asks her to step forward and then pulls down roughly again on SueAnn's shoulder. This time there is a distinct pop when her jaw goes out of joint, and both she and the technician say, "Oh, no!" and SueAnn steps backward. Why in the blue Jesus does she even have to undergo this exam—she is not yet fifty, which she thought was the customary threshold for beginning the darned procedure. And there is the other thing, the thing she cannot say, and even thinking it is sinful: Who gives a fig if I get cancer, anyway? In some ways, it would be a mercy.

On one wall of the examination room hangs a large poster: Twenty Rules to Live By. Some of these consist of pay-it-forward-type good deeds, but there are also a few fun ones, like "Visit Paris," and "Drink champagne for no reason." But the last rule delivers an emotional blow nearly strong enough to again wrench loose her jaw: "Call your mother." *Kyle, honey, why didn't you?*

When SueAnn arrives home from the mammography center, she takes off her shoes and sits down for an iced tea and the afternoon newspaper before Gilbert comes home from work. The *Hope Springs Clarion* is an afternoon daily she counts on for the local scuttlebutt. But today the newspaper has instead published Tulsa news on the front page. She learns that in three weeks a time capsule will be opened in Tulsa, marking Oklahoma's centennial. A portion of this time capsule project in 1957 included burying a '57 Plymouth Belvedere in front of Tulsa's county courthouse, and the car is to be publicly exhumed on June fifteenth. A picture of the pre-burial car appears above the news story. The photo is black and white, but the story reveals that the auto is actually painted gold. A gold car with fins, a '50s American car, like something Elvis might have owned, even if he was a Cadillac man. Though she was not born until 1962, SueAnn has always felt a great nostalgia for the '50s. Sure, she knows about HUAC and all the other stuff, but also there were malt shops and sock hops and strapless gowns with netting and crinolines, and wonderful musicals like

Oklahoma! and *Carousel*. Poor Elvis had not yet ended up on the bathroom floor at Graceland with his pants around his ankles.

I'm going, she decides. I'm taking a vacation day from the Dollar Thrift-O and I'm driving to Tulsa to watch the gold Belvedere be dug up. Kyle would have loved this so much; they could have gone to the event together. But her son, too, rests in an underground vault. And that's a fact, Jack.

Over dinner, Gilbert gives SueAnn the silent treatment. Her husband does not approve of her attending the Wednesday night suicide survivors group. For one thing, he prefers not to acknowledge the suicide of their son; he has made clear his belief that one should not "wallow." For another, he thinks therapy groups are foolishness and hokum. As far as Gilbert is concerned, the fact that the therapist is from San Francisco and two of the other participants are from the East and West Coasts points directly to the airy-fairy nature of the activity. Not only that: Gilbert is miffed about her missing the Wednesday night Bible study meetings, though she still goes to church Sunday mornings and evenings. As she begins clearing the table, Gilbert finally speaks.

"You could just talk to Pastor Russ once in a while," he says. "What's wrong with Oklahoma people? And what's wrong with trusting in the Lord for help?" He pours himself a cup of coffee, splashing the tablecloth. "Next thing, you'll *go Hollywood*, come home wearing them big sunglasses like I seen your doctor wearing."

SueAnn says nothing, but she thinks, *saw*. She attended Tulsa Community College for only one semester, but she tries to better herself, and she has come to realize she has always been smarter than Gilbert, anyway. Sometimes when she comes home from the therapy group, SueAnn goes straight to the computer and googles some of the words Dr. Jane and David and Holly have bandied about during an evening session. They use words like "paradigm" and "synchronicity," and once Dave even said something about hegemony, which at first SueAnn had been unable to find online, as she had not known how to spell the word. They do not talk down to her or indicate that they think she is dumb; rather, they assume she is following their conversations, when in fact sometimes she is not. She usually sits next to her fellow Oklahoman, a widower named Clay who drives down from Ponca City once a week for the meetings. She senses an unspoken bond between them: they do not see "Okie" as a dirty word. SueAnn still remembers what Connie Chung said when she came to Oklahoma City after the bombing. Chung had been overheard calling Oklahoma "backward," motivating some construction workers to spray paint the Porta-Potties at the bombing site "Connie Chung's office."

Gilbert glares at her, apparently waiting for her to say something.

"Pastor Russ is a good man," she says, "and I do turn to the Lord, but there's something about being with other people who have, you know . . ."

"It's morbid!" Gilbert says, pushing himself away from the table and leaving the kitchen with his coffee. She cannot reproach Gilbert for not wanting to think of Kyle's death; Gilbert was the one who found their fifteen-year-old son in the garage and had to cut him down.

SueAnn picks up the remote and switches on the TV in the adjacent family room—a phrase that stings, now that her only child is gone—so she can occupy her mind while she washes the dishes. She has been advised in the grief support group that anything is better than letting the mind "run the same tapes over and over again." Dog the Bounty Hunter's leonine head takes up the entire television screen, his bleached and mulleted pompadour blowing in the Kona breeze as he drives a criminal to the hoosegow. Dog begins to philosophize, as he often does just before he turns in bail jumpers.

"It's just like what happened in Romeo and Joliet," Dog says. The criminal in the car stares ahead impassively. SueAnn knows Joliet is a prison; Dr. Jane would say something about Dog's frame of reference. Dog Chapman's muscular arms are massive as redwood trunks and adorned with armlets and bracelets. Her husband would never wear jewelry, but she can remember when his biceps were as enormous as Dog's. She was only twenty when she married Gilbert Smith, and with his high Choctaw cheekbones and thick black hair, at the time he was the most dazzling man she had ever seen. In those days oil-rig men were still considered particularly desirable catches, and Gilbert had been a roughneck in Houston and had also worked a couple of times on a derrick fire crew with Red Adair.

If Gilbert is balding and if his powerful arms have gone soft and his hard abdomen morphed into a beer gut, she has dimpling on her rump and her breasts have begun heading south. At least I wear an underwire, she thinks, a rarity in Hope Springs. In the Dollar Thrift-O, she daily observes women wearing polyester pants and voluminous flowered shirts, the women's breasts drooping close to their waists because they wear cheap cotton bras with no wire.

Gilbert is hammering something in the basement, so after she finishes the dishes and turns off the TV, SueAnn opens the door at the top of the stairs and calls down that she will be back a bit after nine. She hustles out of the house, not wanting to be late for the grief support meeting. I'm going to keep mum tonight, she decides, not feeling up to undergoing scrutiny. Dave will probably do most of the talking in any case; the New Yorker has an opinion about everything.

SueAnn opens the door of the Silverado and climbs into the driver's seat and snaps a Hank Jr. CD into the player. She once expected more for her life; when she was young, no one could have convinced her that she would work in Dollar Thrift-O and drive a truck. As a girl she never dreamed of being a supermodel or a singer in Nashville, but she assumed her destiny was something a little grander than being a store clerk. Though she feels a bit disloyal for another of her yearnings, it is also true that she imagined ending up somewhere other than Oklahoma. But she never took the fantasy far enough to imagine where she would go and who or what might possibly take her to someplace like California or New York. She did, though, imagine she would have many children, not that she would have to wait ten years to carry a baby to term and that she would never again conceive. She would especially not have expected to outlive her own offspring. As she starts the truck's engine, she pretends for a moment that she is driving a Plymouth Belvedere, a golden car with glamorous fins like a shark on wheels, her son sitting in the passenger seat, singing along with Hank Jr. in Kyle's recently changed voice, a smooth, pure tenor.

A few months before he did it, Kyle had excused himself from the dinner table, saying he needed to do some research on the 'net for a report about the 1950s he was writing for his history class. "I don't know why they think we should care about any of that crap," he complained as he scuffed away from the table.

SueAnn had said, "Don't cuss," overlapping Gilbert as he said, "Watch your mouth, or do you think you're too old for the strap, sport?"

Half an hour later SueAnn knocked on Kyle's bedroom door but entered before he said come in. Her son was hunched over the computer, his head framed by the Kid Rock concert poster on the wall, wearing headphones and the black hoodie that made him look like one of the street thugs pictured on the front of his rap CDs. Her philosophy was: Don't fight with teens about clothing or music—save your energy for the big stuff. Glancing up at her, Kyle swiftly minimized the screen on his Mac, then shut down the computer entirely. He tipped one of the headphones away from his ear with a rough gesture.

"Knock loud!" he said, his sullen face inflamed as much from acne as annoyance, the poor kid. Inexplicably, she heard a Bill Haley song emanating from his headphones, muffled but recognizable, *I'm gonna rock I'm gonna rock*. Kyle bared his teeth at her like a growling dog.

Vexation overtook SueAnn as suddenly as a May tornado, and she found herself lurching forward and pulling down her son's black hood, yanking the headphones from his ears. "Don't sass me!" she said, and when Kyle only smirked and reached to pick up the headphones, she struck him on the shoulder and blurted, "You're a bad news bear!" She hit him a second time, harder, then left the bedroom as hastily as possible, too ashamed to apologize.

The truck runs out of gas shortly after SueAnn leaves the house, making her more than half an hour late for the grief support group. She has to wonder if Gilbert left the tank empty to sabotage her. As she walks into the church fellowship hall, SueAnn glances into a room off the hallway, a room Dave told her serves as an A.A. meeting place. She hears people laughing intemperately, followed by myriad simultaneous fits of coughing. She knows that many recovering alcoholics smoke heavily, trading away their lungs for their livers. Even in the hallway, she can smell the strong aroma of burning coffee. Another burst of loud laughter—what on earth is so funny about alcoholism?

She hurries past the recovering drinkers and into her own meeting room, where she takes the empty chair next to Clay.

"I didn't even know Reed had a gun," Holly says. "My god, it was an enormous shotgun—where did he manage to hide the thing?"

Dr. Jane looks over at SueAnn, but does not smile or wink at her as she usually does when SueAnn arrives. The rebuke is minimal, but SueAnn realizes she is being scolded for her tardiness.

Holly says nothing more after her rhetorical question and sits with a vacant expression on her face. After a few moments of silence in the room, Dr. Jane says, "SueAnn, has anything come up for you this week that you'd like to share with us?"

The words fly from SueAnn's mouth; her vow of silence seems to have had no legs. "I can't take Gilbert's disapproval anymore," she says. "Since we lost Kyle, Gilbert's like a bully."

Dave asks if she has tried to talk with her husband about his behavior.

"He would never tell me what's bugging him, even if he knew what it was," SueAnn says. Everyone looks at her, waiting for clarification. She continues. "If Kyle had shot himself like Holly's fiancé did, things wouldn't be so hard for Gil."

Holly flinches sharply in her chair and says, "What do you mean?"

"It's the fact that Kyle hung himself that Gilbert can't handle," SueAnn says. "He just don't—he doesn't think that's very manly, though he's never really said so. And there's been talk in town that maybe Kyle was hanging himself for a sexual thrill." SueAnn knows what she does not now reiterate: Kyle's hanging was not an act of autoeroticism gone wrong or any other kind of accident; he left a note.

Dr. Jane spends several minutes making a few generic replies to SueAnn's comment, but no one else says anything further. After a bit, Dave speaks. "I tried the Viagra," he says, blushing deeply and looking at his lap. No one says anything, not even Dr. Jane, who looks down at her wristwatch, and the silence seems to go on for a long time. Then Dr. Jane says, "It's nine o'clock—we'll have to pick up next Wednesday." Everyone immediately stands, the scraping of chairs on the floor the only sound in the room.

Pastor Russ is off on a rant against homosexuals, again. The minister is preaching to the choir, all right, SueAnn thinks. Every time he says the word "abomination," there is a flurry of nodding among the congregation and a few utterances of "Praise Jesus" and "Amen." Gilbert sits uncharacteristically still next to her in the pew, not fidgeting or scratching himself as he often does during the sermon. He is an active guy, and sitting motionless does not come naturally to him. She knows Gilbert agrees with Pastor Russ's condemning remarks against homosexuals and that he is profoundly disturbed by the note Kyle left. "My own son, a fairy" was her husband's initial response to Kyle's note. She knows she is neither a good enough Christian nor a worthy enough human being to be able to forgive such disloyalty toward their child. And Gilbert most certainly does not want anyone in town to know about the note and its revelations. He tore up the sheet of paper before the 911 responders arrived.

"Leviticus 20:13!" shouts Pastor Russ, waving his arms in a manner that SueAnn cannot help but think of as stagy. He pulls a crimped handkerchief from his breast pocket and wipes at his brow. Since Kyle died, more and more frequently she senses that nothing around her is authentic, that everything might be a giant con. Pastor Russ continues: "If a man also lie with mankind, as he lieth with a woman, both of them have committed an abomination: they shall surely be put to death! Their blood shall be upon them!"

SueAnn figured out long ago that what is accepted as fact is often just not true. "Ain't Necessarily So" has always been her favorite song from Porgy and Bess. When Pastor Russ begins railing against the homosexuals, she sometimes fantasizes that Libby Payne, the organist and vocalist, might suddenly launch into the song, her tight red curls bobbing up and down as she pounds the keyboard, knocking the congregation off kilter. But she knows Libby would be more likely to sprout horns than do something like that, and probably no one in the chapel shares SueAnn's secret doubts about Scripture. People call Oklahoma the Bible Belt, which SueAnn finds an accurate description. Belts can be good—they keep one's pants where they belong. But belts can also be used as a garrote.

She joins the congregation in singing "I Know That My Redeemer Liveth," her mind absenting the chapel. At the time she gave birth to Kyle, the obstetrical community, particularly in a rural town like Hope Springs, still entertained some odd ideas about infant development. She remembers being told that babies were born blind; that the smiles of a newborn were not smiles at all, but crude reflexes or even gas on the stomach; that babies could not comprehend anything adults said to them. She had always suspected these beliefs were false—heck, her old Australian cow dog could understand everything she said. And in fact Kyle proved SueAnn's suppositions to be correct. Two seconds after he was born, he grabbed the stethoscope out of the doctor's hand, instigating a roar of surprised laughter in the delivery room. *Some blind kid*, SueAnn remembers thinking. And her baby son knew the word "bottle" when he was only a few weeks old. She would say, "Are you ready for your bottle?" and he would turn his flossy head, hyper alert, an expression of undeniable awareness in his clear blue eyes, an old soul. *Oh, Kyle.*

Sometimes in her heart of hearts, SueAnn cannot help but have a particularly wicked thought. What if Pastor Russ is a homosexual himself. Maybe he's like that pastor in Colorado, Ted Haggard, or even like that senator in the airport men's room. Those guys had played people like a two-dollar banjo. She looks closely at Pastor Russ, looking for traces of effeminacy, but sees none. But Kyle was not effeminate, either. Though he said in his note that he had come to realize his sin of homosexuality, SueAnn thinks probably her son was just confused. Wasn't fifteen too young to know whether you were homosexual or not? She wishes he had been able to talk with her about things. *Call your mother.* The sad reality, though, is that at the time she probably would have referred him to Pastor Russ for counseling. She closes her eyes. *Jesus, please give me strength, Lord.*

Just after SueAnn rings up an elderly man's purchase of tube socks and a two-pack of white boxer shorts, she sees that Holly from the grief support group is the next person in line. Funny, she had not really thought of Holly as someone who would shop at a bargain store—she's from the West Coast and has always looked to be on the rich side. SueAnn feels the heat of a blush overtaking her neck and face. What is the proper protocol, she wonders, for greeting someone you know only from a therapy setting?

"SueAnn!" Holly says, "How nice to see you—especially away from the

Suicide Club." She laughs as giddily as the reformed drunks at the Bethel Baptist fellowship hall.

Taken aback by the flippant reference to the support group, SueAnn fumbles with the items she rings up for Holly: exfoliating towelettes, a corkscrew, a plastic bathtub duckie, a Steely Dan CD, and four scented candles. "That will be eight-seventy," she says. "It's nice to see you, too, Holly."

Not knowing what else to say, as she bags Holly's purchases, SueAnn asks, "Are you going to group tomorrow night?"

"Yeah, I think so," Holly replies. "But there's something else I've been wondering about. Are you planning to go to Tulsa to see the Belvedere dug up?"

SueAnn cannot imagine why Holly has asked her this, but she answers semi-truthfully: "I haven't decided for sure."

A heavyset woman wearing a cropped T-shirt bearing the phrase *Oregon: the Beaver State* has stepped in front of Holly and places a basket of items on the counter, so SueAnn only smiles as Holly says, "We'll talk later," and turns to leave.

What in the Sam Hill does an L.A. woman like Holly want to do with the Oklahoma centennial time capsule? If she was hinting that they ought to drive to Tulsa together, SueAnn is not sure what she thinks about the proposal. How do you feel about that? Dr. Jane might ask—the shrink's default inquiry. I don't know. I don't know how I feel about anything.

"You might could get that took care of," Belly Shirt says, pointing to SueAnn's head.

SueAnn is mute, wondering what's wrong with her head—or is it her hair?

"Your earlobes are nearly tore through," the woman says. "The one on your right side is ninety-nine percent ripped out. That happened to my cousin—you need to get it fixed by a doctor."

"Thank you," SueAnn says. This answer is part of the Dollar Thrift-O employee policy: *Just say thanks.* But she feels her stomach eddy with resentment. Forgive me, God, for malicious feelings.

After the woman leaves, SueAnn touches her earlobes, fingering the long slits that used to be tiny holes. Twenty years of wearing heavy earrings have pulled down her earlobes, turning the pierced holes into unsightly slots, clefts that sometimes bead up with blood if she tries to wear earrings. She had not really realized that other people might notice. Good Lord, another body-maintenance chore; she does not need this.

"It's about time to hit the hay, isn't it?" Gilbert says.

SueAnn picks up her sewing basket and says, "I'll be in as soon as I finish up with my mending." If she plays her cards right, SueAnn can usually time things so that bedtime works out for her. If Gil begins yawning and seems as if he is ready to call it a night, she comes up with a chore she needs to do or a phone call she has to make. Though she says she'll join him soon, she will not approach the bedroom until she is sure she hears him snoring. Conversely, if Gilbert goes out bowling with the guys, or if he is working on a project in the basement, she goes to bed early, and if she is not actually asleep when her husband comes to bed, she has learned how to seem asleep. Gilbert now goes off to the bedroom without saying anything more. She is ashamed that she has at times gone even further with her deception, every now and then pretending to have a yeast infection, drawing out the bogus malady for a week or two to avoid sexual contact.

At first, in the months after Kyle's death, she figured her loss of desire was probably caused by grief. Then, when her doctor put her on an antidepressant, he told SueAnn that sometimes antidepressants suppressed the libido. Gilbert pressed for sex the first few months of her loss of desire, followed by insults about menopausal women. The situation has plateaued so that now she has to deal with sexual issues only if she and Gilbert happen to go to bed at the same time—assuming he is not in a snit about the grief support group, in which case he turns his back to her.

SueAnn has considered that Gilbert could be correct—that the erotic time of her life has come and gone and she is now a dried-up crone. She has also entertained the thought that the antidepressant really has damped down her desire. But how to explain, then, the surge of heat she feels in her pelvis when she watches that Dr. McDreamy on TV or sees a movie starring Joaquin Phoenix before he went mental.

Suicide wreaks holy havoc on a survivor's sexual life. SueAnn has not brought up "the problem" in her therapy group, even though Dave has been very upfront about his erectile dysfunction since his father died, and Holly has confessed to erotic cravings for her fiancé that have ghoulishly persisted beyond the grave. Clay just shakes his head grimly when asked about sex and will say nothing. For a while a twenty-two-year-old girl in the group, whose boyfriend had killed himself, was acting out sexually: going to the bars every night and finding herself in a strange bed nearly every morning. Once she even woke up in an alley behind a bar, barefooted and with her expensive cowboy boots missing. The girl quit the group after only three weeks.

Maybe, SueAnn tells herself, she will want Gilbert again, someday. Or maybe not, and then she will have to decide what to do about their marriage. She and Gilbert have been married for twenty-five years, and up until now he has always been someone she could lean on. Though his ripping up of Kyle's suicide note wounded SueAnn, the fact is that he also made sure she did not have to see Kyle's broken body, their son's neck askew like the neck of a strangled chicken in her daddy's barnyard. Gilbert had shut the garage door and shepherded SueAnn into the house, and while they waited for the emergency responders, Gilbert sat close to her on the davenport, his arm tight around her trembling shoulders.

She knows this particular memory shouldn't be something she compares to Kyle's death, but SueAnn still recalls when her cow dog, Louie, was run over in the road and killed. Gilbert buried him in a handmade box in the orchard behind their house and hammered a little wooden cross into the ground on Louie's grave. She still loves her husband for that. Poor Gilbert: Kyle's suicide has ravaged Gil's life just as much as hers. The only difference is, he is still unaware that their former life is exactly that. The snoring starts; she can now go to bed.

The traffic in downtown Tulsa is heavy, and SueAnn hopes she does not rear-end someone's car as she watches for street signs that will direct her to the turnpike back to Hope Springs. She is not accustomed to driving in the metro area, and she feels embarrassed to be driving a truck, as the folks in Tulsa seem mostly to be driving SUVs or tank-size sedans.

She is making her way home after an afternoon visit to a plastic surgeon—something that is not available in Hope Springs. SueAnn was surprised, when she asked her family doctor about the torn earlobes, to be referred to the plastic surgeon. Turns out, the holes in her lobes could not just be sewn up. They had to first be reamed out, made even larger, followed by a stitching up of the new wound, which should heal over the original slits. If she wants to continue to wear ear wires, she will have to be re-pierced. There was no pain during the procedure, nor do her earlobes hurt now. But the surgeon taped square white bandages on each ear, and SueAnn now resembles her next door neighbor's Great Dane after he had his ears docked. She does not look forward to the stares that will come her way tomorrow at the Dollar Thrift-O.

As she turns onto the road leading to the turnpike, she glances inside a car driving parallel to her truck, in the next lane over. A woman drives the sedan, and in the back sits a young-teen couple. The boy has his arm around the girl, who sits right next to him. A little date, SueAnn thinks, and the boy is too young to drive, so Mom takes them out. Gosh, she had forgotten about the time she chauffeured Kyle and a girl on a date—Kyle's first and only date, as far as she knows. It was a school dance during Kyle's last year of middle school, and the thirteen-year-old Kyle had asked one of his classmates to be his date, a friendly strawberry-blond girl SueAnn saw again at Kyle's funeral.

So when had Kyle decided he was gay? Did he have "dates" with boys that she was unaware of? Maybe an older boy who drove them somewhere. She cannot imagine such a thing. She has read about adolescent boys having mutual masturbation sessions—could there have been something like that?

Kyle and his date wanted to have dinner before the dance, so SueAnn had driven them to Siesta Sancho's, where she took a table alone, a good distance away from the kids' table for two. She was able to watch them as they studied their menus, talked, laughed, ate soft tacos and drank Cokes, and afterward she drove them to the school gymnasium and dropped them off for the dance.

Well, I'll always have that. I was part of Kyle's first date, and it was perfectly normal and very sweet—no signs of burgeoning homosexuality. Had he been having doubts that early? She will never know. SueAnn reaches into the truck's cup holder, scooping up quarters for the road toll. Her earlobes have begun to throb painfully, and she feels them swelling up, as if two ripe peaches hang from her head.

SueAnn is first to arrive at the grief support group tonight, even before Dr. Jane. She sits down next to the chair where Clay usually sits; maybe he is stuck in traffic on his way from Ponca. Dave comes in a few moments later and sits across from SueAnn.

"Whoa! What the hell happened to you?" Dave says, pointing to the oblong tape covering the lobes of SueAnn's ears.

"I had a procedure," she responds, hoping Dave will leave things at that. She cannot help but feel as if she were wearing a dunce cap. At that moment Holly comes into the room. She glances at SueAnn's bandaged ears and then looks politely away, saying hello before she sits down.

"Clay and Dr. Jane aren't here yet?" Holly says. "The Suicide Club can't go ahead without them."

SueAnn says nothing, not wanting to draw further attention to her throbbing earlobes.

"How did you come up with the name Suicide Club, anyway?" Holly says.

"I didn't invent the name," Dave says. "There was a group in San Francisco called the Suicide Club."

SueAnn is so astonished that she forgets her shyness about her Great Dane ears. "Are you joking?" she says.

"Oh no, no joke," he says. "It started in the seventies out at San Francisco State. My best friend, Phil Shapiro, was one of the founding members. Actually, nowadays they call it the Cacophony Society—they changed the name."

Holly says, "It's a grief support group?"

"No no," Dave says. "Nothing like that. It was a sort of guerilla-theater-type thing, if you're old enough to remember Julian Beck. A bunch of artists who did capers and photographed them—sort of a cross between goofing off and performance art." He adds, "There's something similar now in New York. They call it Improv Everywhere."

SueAnn is not sure she understands, exactly, but she can go on Google later. Holly nods, and at that moment Dr. Jane comes into the room, greeting them and taking her usual chair.

"Clay isn't here?" Jane says.

"Not yet," Dave says. "While we're waiting, we've been talking about a group of artists in San Francisco—they called their association the Suicide Club." He seems to recall that Jane is from San Francisco, and adds, "Do you remember them?"

Dr. Jane frowns and crosses her ankles, shakes her head no.

Dave turns again to Holly and SueAnn. "The odd thing is—and maybe this is one of the reasons they changed the name to Cacophony Society—Phil Shapiro actually did commit suicide, in the eighties, more than ten years after he was a grad student at S.F. State."

No one says anything, but all SueAnn can think is, poor Dave. His best friend and his father both killed themselves. What kind of dark shadow follows him around? She has lived in Oklahoma long enough not to be surprised when lightning strikes more than once in the same place. And she has heard about something called the suicide spell, when people who have been exposed to suicide end up later doing the same thing themselves. SueAnn's high school English teacher said the writer Ernest Hemingway's father killed himself before Hemingway did, and after that a number of other members of the Hemingway family, about half a dozen, including his granddaughter, decades later. Clay enters the room, apologizing for being late, and SueAnn finds herself letting out a breath of what must be relief. Clay has not become another suicide statistic, is alive and well, even if tonight he looks a little gray around the gills.

"No, I'm not going—it's a waste of time," Gilbert says, turning up the volume on the Rangers game on the TV. "The thing will be all messed up, rusted out. No vehicle underground fifty years can survive."

"I've been reading a lot about this in the paper," SueAnn says. "The car's in a vault—like a bank vault or an Egyptian tomb—it's completely watertight."

"Nothing is completely watertight," Gilbert says. "And especially not something built in Tulsa fifty years ago. Why do you think they bury people above ground in New Orleans? Because bodies come floating up out of the 'watertight vaults' if they're put underground."

SueAnn wants to point out that Oklahoma is not below sea level like New Orleans. She does not care to argue at all about the Belvedere—she knows the car will be unharmed, gleaming gold, even now seeming futuristic in its aerodynamic design. If Gilbert will not go with her, she will simply take up Holly on the offer to drive to Tulsa for the unearthing ceremony. The fact is, she and Holly and Dave have begun to fraternize outside the group. Just this Wednesday they went to Sancho's after group, drinking margaritas and sharing nachos, and it was then that Holly offered to drive. In one sense, it's sad that now her only friends are fellow suicide victims, bound together by the worst sort of grief.

This Friday is the day of the Belvedere's exhumation. She goes to the back of the house and into what used to be Kyle's bedroom and calls Holly to confirm the trip to Tulsa.

Holly's voice on her answering machine says drolly, "This is Holly. If you leave a message, maybe I'll call you back." At first SueAnn is taken aback, but then she realizes she prefers this message to the "You have a blessed day, now" that she so often hears on other answering machines in Hope Springs.

SueAnn leaves a message, then logs on to what used to be Kyle's computer. Gil purged the hard disk long before, switched to broadband, and set up a new e-mail account. Nothing remains of their son save a discolored spot on the screen where Kyle had once stuck a Slayer sticker that Gil scraped off.

An impulse causes her to google the Suicide Club San Francisco, wondering if anything will pop up. The first site she clicks on displays a photo of what appears to be a membership card.

The Bearer
has agreed to get all worldly affairs in order,
to enter into the world of Chaos, cacophony & dark saturnalia,
to live each day as if it were the last,
and is a member in good standing of the
Suicide Club

She is surprised when numerous entries pop up. There is of course that whacked-out death cult in Japan, but what interests her is that the organization in San Francisco had nothing whatever to do with suicide. She reads that the group was formed in the late seventies by a guy named Gary Warne and two other guys who had a predilection for lighthearted practical jokes, though there is no mention of Dave's friend Shapiro. The club developed into a group of people who performed street theater. Examples given include riding a cable car en masse, entirely naked. Another time they set up a small table in an elevator in a San Francisco business-district high rise, quickly setting a formal dinner service—complete with white linen and a floral centerpiece—and sitting down to dine on plates of garden salad accompanied by glasses of wine. When the elevator opened on the ground floor of the building, a gaggle of stone-faced lawyers and stockbrokers stood stock still and staring.

She scrolls downward, reading a blurb by one of the founding members: "Have you ever explored a subterranean sewer at night with forty other people; climbed three storeys on a swinging rope ladder to dine on the roof of a condemned building; shared the surreal experience of being in a group of people scaling the Golden Gate Bridge in the fog?"

Another posting declares: "You may already be a member. Are you a: squeak in the door of normalcy; a dada clown rewiring the neural circuits of the community; a happy dog rolling on the carcass of preconceptions?" Maybe not, SueAnn thinks, but maybe I might have been, if I'd been born somewhere else. Heat sears her chest, along with a grim realization, something she has never before considered: Kyle would not have killed himself if he had been born in a place like San Francisco, a place of infinite possibility. She prints out the membership card and slips it into the pocket of her sweater.

She reads that the core of the group's philosophy was inspired by the writer William Blake's statement "The road of excess leads to the palace of wisdom."

"Have you heard about that new diet pill called Alli?" Holly says.

"I've seen it at Walmart," SueAnn responds.

SueAnn sits in the passenger seat of Holly's vintage Mustang convertible. They are driving to the metro to see the gold Belvedere dug up. There have been media reports that earlier this week during the digging process, workers made note of significant water leakage into the vault, and no one is sure how the Plymouth may have fared. Some surmise that the car will be barely blemished, while others predict little but a degraded hull. SueAnn is among the former group, believing that the Plymouth Belvedere will be as intact and golden as the day it was buried, whereas Holly is a glass-is-empty gal and has expressed her doubts.

"I want to lose five pounds," Holly continues, "so I picked up a box of Alli and started reading the label."

SueAnn is astonished. Holly appears to weigh no more than 110 pounds. Why would she go on a diet? She guesses it's a California thing—they all seem so body conscious on the Coast. She nods at Holly, listening.

"Do you know about the diarrhea issue?" Holly says.

"No, I . . ." SueAnn is embarrassed and heat rises from her neck to her face. She feels the way she does when Gilbert's bowling buddies make jokes about flatulence.

Holly continues, "Well, the warning on the label says the stuff can cause what they call 'anal seepage,' and they suggest you wear dark clothing! Can you imagine?"

While Holly laughs to beat the band, SueAnn thinks: What I never could have imagined has nothing to do with pooping my pants. I would never in a trillion and two years have imagined that I would be driving along the Arkansas River in a convertible with the top down, with a hip, educated woman like Holly, a bookstore owner who talks about Faulkner and Nietzsche and Proust as if they're pals—a woman from California. Though SueAnn and Holly have become friendly, SueAnn feels like a rube around her and has even had to wonder why Holly wants to be friends. Maybe it's as simple as that Holly often wants to talk about her dead boyfriend and SueAnn is always willing to listen.

"God!" Holly says. "How great would it be if I'm wrong and the Belvedere really is hauled up in nearly all its former glory? Cars were so glamorous in the fifties, you know?" She laughs again, clearly euphoric, and

SueAnn recalls Holly mentioned upping the dosage on her antidepressant. Holly is probably a bit intoxicated by the medication.

"I've seen those cars in movies," SueAnn says. "Like in *Giant*. And I've seen them on a *60 Minutes* show about Cuba. They all drive 1950s cars down there."

Holly snaps on the car's CD player and out blasts Ike Turner singing "Rocket 88." She says, "To set the tone," then adds, "Most people don't know this, but Ike's version came out years before Bill Haley and the Comets'." Holly sings along, straying from Turner's lyrics, "She has a V-8 engine, honey—it's gold and it's fine."

Holly, concerned about car thieves, parks her convertible in a pricey indoor parking structure, and SueAnn and she hoof it the several blocks to the excavation site at Denver and 7th. Before they catch sight of the dig, they see television vans and reporters with microphones. The public has been herded behind a chain link fence erected for the event, and SueAnn and Holly wormhole their way from the back of the crowd, inching as close to the fence as possible.

"They're lifting the lid already," Holly says, grabbing SueAnn's elbow and pulling her along, slithering their way to the second row of people thronging against the fence.

A group of hard-hatted workers lifts the heavy lid of the vault, setting it aside. The mood of the crowd grows even more buoyant, and hoots of excitement speckle the air. After what seems like a long time, equipment-tethered ropes begin to elevate the car itself, though there may be help from a hydraulic device below. When she and Gilbert went to Las Vegas, they saw David Copperfield appear onstage by rising from the floor, slowly, as if ascending from the netherworld. When SueAnn stands on tiptoes, she can see the car rising slowly from the muck, a muddy shroud still clinging to the Belvedere, and her spine actually tingles as the whistling and shouting of the crowd grow louder and more fevered.

"Oh, Christ—she's a doner," a man behind them says, and SueAnn cranes her neck to the side. The tarpaulin has begun to fall away from the car, and what is clear to everyone is that the Plymouth is no longer gold but is a rusted-out hull. In spots the vehicle is mottled the color of mustard, the shade of a jar of Gulden's Spicy Brown.

The Bible says if you have faith the size of a mustard seed, you will have the conviction to say to a mountain, "Move over there." When she went to the Internet after Kyle's death and looked up the parable of the mustard seed, she discovered the Buddhists possess more wisdom on the topic. The Buddha told the story of the grieving mother and the mustard seed. When a mother lost her only son, she took his corpse to the Buddha, seeking a cure. The Buddha asked her to bring a handful of mustard seeds from a family that had never lost a child, husband, parent, or friend. When the mother was unable to find such a house in her village, she realized that death is common to all, and she could not be selfish in her grief. *But I can—I can be very selfish in my grief.*

At Kyle's funeral, after the Twenty-Third Psalm and all the rest of what SueAnn now thinks of as standard bereavement clichés, Pastor Russ read from the book of John. She heard his theatrical voice, though she did not see him, her eyes too swollen to view anything clearly through the dark glasses Gil had begged her not to wear.

"Everyone who believes that Jesus is the Messiah," quoted Pastor Russ, "is born of God. And everyone who loves the father loves his child as well." She was struck then and there, as if a bowling ball had dropped from the chapel ceiling and bashed her in the brainpan. At that moment in the chapel, she felt spite burn through her body like cascading lava, cauterizing her pain and transforming it into rage so potent she could actually smell it. The heavy sweetness of the floral tributes in the Hope Springs Cornerstone Baptist Church chapel in that instant were replaced in SueAnn's nostrils by a malodorous foulness, a smell not unlike the eggish fumes she encountered when her parents took her to the hot sulphur springs in Montana one summer when she was a child.

SueAnn stares at the Belvedere, blinking against the sun. She hears ragged weeping somewhere behind her among the onlookers. In the blinding glare of the Tulsa sun she stands riveted, the Plymouth, twisting beneath its rope tethers, shrouded and defunct. She fumbles in her sweater pocket for her dark glasses, the very same pair she wore at Kyle's funeral, but what she feels instead is the Suicide Club membership card she printed the other evening. She fingers the paper in her pocket and seems able to read it without looking, as if some sort of sorcery has raised the letters like Braille: *The bearer has agreed to enter into the world of chaos and cacophony and is a member in good standing of the Suicide Club.*

FUBAR

Give . . . wine unto those that be of heavy hearts.
Let him drink, and forget his poverty,
and remember his misery no more.

Proverbs 31:6–7

At LAX on his way to the gate, Slater slips on something and nearly bumps into a young woman with an orange tan, wearing backless high-heeled shoes and accompanied by a Yorkie on a rhinestone leash. She stands talking into an iPhone, blocking the flow of foot traffic, stock still, right in front of one of those airport news shops. As she inexplicably holds the phone in front of her face, smiles, and snaps her own photo, Slater stops to examine the bottom of his shoe and determines he has stepped in dog crap.

The woman does not notice or pretends not to notice her dog has defecated, so as Slater walks on he says, "Excuse me! Your dog pooped here!" For a moment she lifts her chin and meets Slater's glance, but then looks away. By this time Slater has passed her, so he calls over his shoulder, "Don't foul the footpath!"

He's on his way back to Oklahoma, having just spent the weekend in Santa Monica, most recently photographing Frank Gehry's residence. Beth was unable to come along on the trip, needing to act as hostess for a long-planned baby shower for one of her friends' daughters, which is the primary reason he chose this particular weekend—he does not want her or anyone else to find out about the real deal, the thing that *actually* brought him to Southern California. Well, the old saw is true, it only hurts when he laughs, so he made sure last night not to watch any comedies on the hotel-room television. He looks at his watch and realizes he has time to kill. Might as well grab an early lunch. He heads for the bar where he knows he can order a quick burger and a double Manhattan.

When he takes a seat, the surge of pain stuns Slater. His entire torso thrums with a burning ache. Must be the elastic pressure belt the surgeon has made him wear. How will he be able to hide the thing from Beth? It's not as if coming to bed with a girdle on is something that heretofore has been within the realm of possibility. He stifles the groan he feels on the verge of emitting and orders a Rusty Nail. Where did that come from? He has not drunk a scotch and Drambuie since he was young and still teaching at Pratt, and he fully intended to order his usual Manhattan. The pain must have called up a weird unconscious association—there is something toxic sounding about a rusted nail, the taint of tetanus. *Discomfort*, my ass.

The woman to his left turns her face ever so slightly away from Slater as she reads the *Los Angeles Times* and sips a glass of white wine. Don't worry, I'm not going to land on you, Slater thinks. It occurs to him that maybe she smells dog do, so he leans down and wipes off his shoe, then rolls up the paper napkin and wings it over the bar and into a garbage receptacle. He thanks the bartender for the drink and takes a long pull on the Rusty Nail. The slow heat from his throat to his chest provides a winning contrast to the ugly burn tearing through his torso—his "core," as the guys in the gym now say.

What would his father say if he had lived to know that his only son had plunked down beaucoup bucks to have fat sucked and lasered from his midsection? The answer could not be clearer: Poppy would say his son had turned into a vain ponce, that no real man would spend money on womanly medical procedures. But his father also claimed that any man who would commit suicide had to be a "sister man"—that only a sissy would be too afraid to live. "When the going gets tough, the tough get going," his father often said, and at times employed other 1950s clichés, such as "A quitter never wins and a winner never quits," truisms that even then Slater viewed as tired pap and an offshoot of social Darwinism, not what one might expect from a hardcore labor union man like his dad. As for Poppy deliberately overdosing on sleeping pills, Slater might more easily have predicted him joining the Taliban, or having a sex change operation, or even becoming a Republican.

But Poppy was always a complex guy, no doubt about that. He had been for the most part a kind and doting father when Slater was a kid, taking him to Dodgers games and fishing at Breezy Point jetty and even serving as Cubmaster to his Cub Scout pack. He called his son Davey-Man or Slugger and never missed one of Slater's baseball games or soccer matches. He hired a metal band for Slater's bar mitzvah party, a downer for the oldsters but bliss for Slater and the other thirteen-year-olds. But as a father he had a dark side, too, what Slater's grief counselor called a "Jungian shadow." He could become sadistic, without warning and for no apparent reason. When Slater was going through his cowboy phase in the first grade, his very favorite song was the country standard "Red River Valley"—ironic now that he has ended up living in Oklahoma. One day young Slater was sitting at the kitchen table in their flat when they still lived in Flatbush, drawing with crayons on butcher paper. Another of Poppy's contradictions: he played piano beautifully and even composed his own music, not what you might think of as your standard-issue longshoreman. Slater had at times sat next to Poppy on the piano bench, watching him play. On the day of the coloring crayons, David had drawn wobbly lines across the page and was drawing crude replicas of what he thought looked like musical notes.

"How 'bout that!" Poppy had exclaimed. "Did you know you've written down the music for 'Red River Valley'?"

Slater can still remember the astonished pleasure resulting from his father's revelation. At six years of age, not once had he considered that his father would tell him anything untrue—this possibility had never entered his mind. With the magical thinking of young children, accepting that he had accidentally duplicated his favorite piece was conceivable, in some giddy, unanticipated way.

But Poppy had not been content to leave the joke there, inside their family flat. His father insisted that David take the piece to school with him the next day, tell the teacher that the crayoned page contained the song "Red River Valley," and ask her to play the tune on the piano to the class during music time. Feeling shy, David had said he did not want to, but Poppy insisted. The inevitable had happened: Slater took the sheet to the young, freckled woman who was his first-grade teacher, explained that it contained "Red River Valley," and earnestly requested that she play the song during music time. Slater does not remember everything about his life as a six-year-old, but this moment has a grotesque clarity. The teacher's facial expression had gone from surprised to blank to contemplative, and then she told him sweetly that she had something else planned for today, but that she would try to play the piece some other time. That had been satisfactory to David, but when he arrived home that evening, his father immediately asked if the teacher played the cowboy song for the class. When Slater reported on the events, his father laughed long and hard, his wolfish teeth flashing. Not until many years later did Slater recall the incident and realize his father had punked him.

Conversely, Poppy had brought up his kids to do the right thing, and in particular never to lie. And Slater never has been a liar, has always aimed to be a mensch. But ever since Poppy killed himself, Slater has found himself in uncharted waters. Though he cannot get it up with Beth, he lusts inappropriately after women in his circle; he skips his office hour sometimes and leaves students in the lurch; and last, but certainly not least, he skulks off to California and has liposuction. While it is true that plenty of straight guys have "procedures" these days, Slater never imagined that he would be one of those men.

He does not really give a damn whether the woman next to him at the bar knows what he has done, so he removes from the inside pocket of his jacket the brochure the surgeon's assistant gave him when he left the surgery suite Friday.

After a surgery like liposuction, patients may be bloated and feel distended. Liposuction surgery is really a controlled injury—body fluid rushes to the site and the injured tissue becomes like a sponge. Your physician has gone under the carpet of skin and taken away the fat undercoating, so the raw surface oozes serum on the inside.

Before he came to Santa Monica for the lipo, he studied up on the procedure and probably should have decided then and there not to go ahead with it. When he read the Internet info, all he could think of was the liquefaction that takes place after a serious earthquake. During the Loma Prieta earthquake in '89, because San Francisco's Marina District had been built upon superficial sandy materials that were used to fill the old lagoon in 1915, liquefaction had caused water-saturated fine-grain sands and silts to behave as viscous fluids rather than solids. This liquidity caused entire buildings to sink into the muck. Slater's flesh feels equally unstable, roiling and suppurating beneath the pressure belt.

He chugs most of his drink and tries to catch the eye of the bartender, then pulls a notebook from his attaché case. Making lists has for Slater become like yoga for many others; the process calms his nerves and evens him out. He thinks for a moment, then writes:

THINGS ABOUT L.A.:

Surprisingly good buildings—Santa Monica Heritage Museum kind of cool

Breast implants ubiquitous, even the hotel maids

Very, very white teeth

Bartenders and waitresses ready for their close-up

Armpits on display—sleeves at a premium

Hug each other constantly, just like on Leno

What he should make is a list of ideas about how to hide the lipo from Beth. It's not as if he could claim that he had undergone the procedure on a spur-of-the moment impulse just because he happened to be in Santa Monica—she would know that one has to schedule this sort of thing in advance, which he had. And maybe the worst part, the part that would be the coup de grâce, is the financial aspect of the caper. He paid more than $7,000 for so-called "smart lipo." He borrowed from his 403b and had all the paperwork routed to his box on campus, but he is not so foolish as to expect that he will not be caught out by Beth someday. As for the bruising, well, he'll just have to remove the pressure belt at night and sleep in a T-shirt. There isn't much chance of them having sex, anyway.

He slides the notebook back into his attaché case and pulls out a stack of mail that he grabbed from his box before he left Hope Springs. There's this week's *Nation*—he'll have something to read on the plane on the way home. And there are the usual bills. But most of the mail he receives these days seems to come from only four sources: the AARP, though he refuses to join; hearing aid companies; burial insurance companies; and funeral directors. When he opens a brochure from one of the burial insurance companies, out falls a return postcard that the recipient is invited to return to the company, asking for more information. He scrawls at the bottom of the postcard: "Remove me from your mailing list. And while you're at it, drop dead yourself."

"Oh! Do you go to Dr. Beauchamp, too?"

The attractive woman on the stool next to him has tapped him on the arm and is smiling like a killer, displaying her lovely teeth, probably porcelain veneers from the looks of them.

Slater is caught off guard. "How'd you . . .?"

She points to the lipo brochure, which has Dr. Beauchamp's name and address printed on it, and Slater nods, not knowing what to say.

"Dr. Mike is my plastic surgeon, too!" she says. "I had my thighs done."

Slater exerts a tremendous effort not to look down at her thighs. "I guess that makes us homeys, then," he says, raising his glass to her. She clinks her wine glass against his nearly empty Rusty Nail.

"Did he give you anything for the pain?" she says. Her gaze morphs into a feral stare.

Oh Lord—he gets it now—all she wants is to score some Vicodin off him. He does not wait for her to ask, just pulls the bottle from the pocket of his blazer, snaps off the lid with his thumb, hands off one tab to the woman and washes down another with his cocktail.

She emits a husky laugh, extends one slim, tanned hand to shake Slater's hand, and with the other hand pops the Vico and washes it quickly down with wine. He notices she has those long, squared-off fingernails he has seen a lot of in L.A.

"I'm Stella," she says.

"Stella by Starlight," Slater says—always one of his favorite songs.

She looks at him with a frown of incomprehension. "I'm sorry?"

Shite, it's the age gap again. She must be part of the Diddy generation, or at best a Michael Bublé fan. Well, never mind. "Another round for the lady and me," Slater tells the barkeep.

Slater wakes just as the plane begins its descent to Will Rogers. He remembers missing his flight from LAX, a flurry of phone calls home, and catching an evening flight, but the time between his leaving the airport bar and getting on the plane is a tad blurry. His last clear memory is of looking at the LAX sign from the plane window as they took off. Yes, he has been *lax*, no doubt about that.

Apparently he fell asleep soon after he took his seat on the flight home. He had managed to get the window, and the middle seat remained miraculously empty. The little old lady on the aisle has already unbuckled her seatbelt and looks as if she wants to vault for the door. Old gal probably has a weak bladder. The sky outside the window is black, though his original flight was to have landed in the afternoon.

Face it, Slater, you went on a bender. He would have guessed, had he even thought about such a thing, that his days of benders were over, not to mention that picking up strange women was a thing of the long ago past, when he was still single. But one thing he does remember from the late sixties and early seventies is that drugs and alcohol have a way of making strange bedfellows. Not that he and the woman at LAX made it to bed— *thank you Jesus*, as Oklahomans are wont to say. But a series of nearly unfathomable events went down in that airport bar, this much he does remember. There was the Vicodin and the second round of cocktails. There were still more cocktails after that, followed by a highly, highly ill-advised second Vicodin each, at which point they vacated their bar stools and moved to a small table in the back of the bar. And, yes! they made out, and apparently made out for hours, as he and Stella both missed their flights.

He remembers the taste of vanilla and the scent of jasmine—God, it was a feast of the senses, and he has a shameful memory of fondling the woman's breasts, and even of her giving him some crotch action. Jesus, from where has all this come? There's that phrase you hear all the time now, "spiraling out of control." Well, he spiraled, all right, big-time. At the same moment that he flushes with shame, his oozing torso begins to throb beneath the pressure belt. He reaches into the breast pocket of his jacket and pulls out the Vicodin container, opens it and tips it toward his palm. Holy crap, only two pills remain! He had at least twenty-five when he entered the airport this morning. Stella must have weaseled the rest out of him—he's been rolled. Reflexively he checks his wallet. While there is no cash left, that is not exactly surprising. Cocktails at the airport bar were an unprecedented eighteen bucks a pop. His credit cards are all there; at least there's that. He swallows a pill without water, the tablet scraping against his throat.

After his elderly row-mate has made it to the aisle and started moving forward, Slater wrenches his bag from beneath the seat in front of him and scooches out to deplane. The pain of his sluicing midsection is nothing when compared to the anguish that overtakes him now as he steps from the plane and back into his real life. He remembers that acronym FUBAR. Yes, his situation now is *fucked up beyond all repair*. At fifty-nine and having been married for more than thirty of those years, he has learned that after crossing certain bridges, there is no way back, period, end of story, that's all she wrote. And the fact is, he has never before cheated on Beth, understanding from the get-go that to do so would change things so irreparably that there would be no recovery. Enough damage to their marriage was done in the early seventies during the *Bob & Carol & Ted & Alice* days, when he and Beth had experimented a bit sexually, but at least then they had both been in on the poor decisions and bad behavior. Recovering from that folly had taken years. But does necking in the airport really count as cheating? It seems more like momentary foolishness he should just forget about. He steps onto the escalator going down to the parking garage, his bag feeling as if it weighs ten stone, his torso vibrating with pain. He has ninety minutes' driving time between OKC and Hope Springs during which he has to think of a way to hide two huge misdemeanors from Beth: the lipo and the interlude with Stella. No, don't even think of her name ever again. Take a page from Slick Willy and think of her as "that woman." Better yet: don't think of her at all.

Something edges into Slater's periphery of pain. Not only is his torso on fire, but his feet hurt, too. The sensation of gnawing, throbbing pain in his midsection is now accompanied by a sharp, lancing stinging from his heels. He finds himself limping, hobbled, tottering off the escalator like some decrepit gray-beard.

And now this recollection comes to him, too, rising from the brown-out in which he has found himself: He nearly missed a second flight out of LAX, and only *that woman* checking the time on her cell phone and yelping had alerted him to the imminence of his outbound flight. He'd had to run forty gates, hell for leather, in order to board before the doors shut. Evidently while he was asleep on the plane, blisters formed on his heels, now pulsing with pain and doubtless weeping like the flesh of his midsection. His limping involuntarily slows as he drags himself toward the lot where he parked his car. People push past him impatiently. He can't make it, Slater realizes, shuffling off to the side and leaning against a wall. He is forced to remove his shoes and carry them, like a teenager sneaking back into the house after curfew. He slips his sunglasses out of his pocket and puts them on so he can avoid eye contact with anyone, and limps back to one of the airport shops, where he buys a pair of fleecy little slippers and pulls them onto his battered feet.

Beth is lying on the sofa when Slater lets himself through the front door. No lights are on, but the television disperses a flickering blue glow throughout the living room. He cannot discern whether her eyes are open.

Slater hears the voice of Dr. G., Medical Examiner. "Was it *natural*?" the doctor queries in her high-pitched voice. "Was it *trauma*? Or was it a *combination* of natural and trauma?"

"Bethie?" Slater says. "Are you awake?"

"Yes," she answers immediately, her voice flat as if she's pissed off.

Off goes the TV, and on goes the lamp on the end table. Over the archway between the living room and dining room hangs a banner several feet wide, consisting of individual plastic letters linked together by pink ribbon, the letters spelling out IT'S A GIRL! For a moment his gut ices over, but then he remembers the baby shower. "How was the party?" he says.

She does not answer, but sits up, points at Slater's feet, and says "What's the deal?"

"Blisters," he says, "bad ones. I had to run for my plane. Bought these at Will Rogers."

"Good grief, Dave, did you have to buy *red* slippers? You look like a clown."

"That's all they had. Left over from the holidays, I guess." He sees now that clinging to the ceiling above Beth's head is a Mylar balloon in the shape of a baby bottle, the nipple a lurid pink.

"How was your trip?" Beth says.

"Okay, but I'm exhausted," he says. "Mechanical trouble with the plane was the last thing I needed." He forces a laugh. "Unless you count blisters."

"Did you see Gehry?"

He says no, that he just shot the house and did some research in the library. "I'm going to take a quick shower and then hit the rack. You coming?" He does not wait for her response but drops his bag and heads for the bathroom, where he can stash the pressure belt in the linen closet and from the hamper scrounge a T-shirt under which to hide the oozing lipo area. He first turns on the hot water, then undresses on the fluffy red bathmat that matches his unfortunate new slippers.

Do I tell her, or not? About either of the things I've done? He decides he needs to sleep on the matter and stoops to pick up his trousers and remove the last Vicodin from a pocket. He steps into the tub, swallows the tab and drinks from the shower, then lets water pound on his head and steam overcome him. He gives himself over to blind sensation, no past no future. *In the here and now,* as they used to say in the sixties.

Slater has already taught his morning seminar and is fulfilling his mandatory afternoon office hour. He hopes no one comes into his office today:

failing students begging for mercy, truants offering trumped up excuses or asking for Incompletes, TAs overwhelmed by their responsibilities, students or former students asking for letters of recommendation—often the very worst students, who if they had any brains would know better than to ask for a rec letter from the professor teaching a course for which they did not earn an A—and the perennial students who just want to talk. These students want badly to secure positions as designers or PAs in good firms as soon as they graduate, or want to bag assistant professorships somewhere. They mistakenly assume he holds the key to how they can succeed in their professional desires. He often offers benign banalities such as "Do your best work—worry about the work, not the rewards," or "Brilliant designs will always rise to the top like cream—be brilliant." He seldom tells them the truth: that maybe one or two students in a section of sixty will ever be good enough to succeed in the private or public sector or academe—that they might as well have gone to trade school in HVAC. Many of them have read *The Fountainhead* and have a weird-ass misperception of what it is to be an architect.

He does still have passion for teaching, and knocks himself out trying to reach the students, to help along the weaker ones by teaching them everything he knows, and to discover the talented ones and help them find their way. But in his less inspired moments, he sometimes feels as if at least some of the time he might be casting pearls before swine.

Being a professor of architecture has changed a great deal since Slater was appointed assistant professor at Pratt nearly thirty years ago. In those days he was still idealistic: oh, visions of Taliesin! At that time 95 percent of his students were male. The few female students were often homely, hairy, serious young women wearing Birkenstocks, who sometimes smelled of onions or of rank perspiration. Things were simpler then. He had very few female students until the 1980s, and until the late 1990s most of the women ended up transferring out of architecture. Now his seminars are packed with bright, often beautiful young women, many of whom shamelessly flirt with him and/or make crude passes. He wasn't trained for this shit. The university offers regular mandated seminars on sexual harassment, but these consist only of trotting out the lawyers, who lecture the professors about how to cover their asses liability-wise. What Slater feels is actually needed is behavioral specialists who teach faculty how to deal with advances from students. It would not hurt, either, if there were some special advice available on how to avoid being attracted to some of these girls. Things are especially complicated these days, since many of the male faculty are taking daily-dose versions of ED meds like Cialis and are likely to pop a woody at inappropriate moments. Slater would likely fall into this category himself, if not for the fact that both Viagra and Cialis give him headaches that feel as if a stiletto and a steel drum are simultaneously at work in his cranium.

He has closed the door to his office, hoping to deter students from coming in. If a student knocks and enters his office, university policy dictates that—whether the student is male or female—professors are to prop their doors open wide so there can be no perception or accusation of sexual impropriety. Students sometimes claim they have been the victim of molestation by professors, and it is also not unheard of for a disgruntled graduate student to come to campus and gun down a professor who declines a dissertation or assigns a failing grade. Three years ago one of his suite mates, a visiting scholar from Rutgers, was shot dead in his office; Slater heard the gun go off. While most often the litigious students or the gun-toters are nut jobs, what is also true is that certain faculty offices are furnished with the equivalent of the Hollywood casting couch. One colleague's office door is closed many hours in the afternoon several times a week, after which a pretty dark-haired young woman is seen to leave the office, carrying an armload of books and wearing a stagy "scholarly" expression on her face. The buzz in the department is that semen stains glow white upon the dark cushions of the guy's office sofa.

Well, who can blame the guy? Isn't Slater sick of his currently sexless existence, the life of a eunuch? When tension builds up to an untenable level, he makes a move on Beth, or submits to one of her advances, but invariably he can't cut the mustard. Things have been this way since the day of Poppy's funeral, and while he understands his dysfunction to be a byproduct of his grief, that awareness does not help the problem in any significant manner. Beth has obviously begun to resent him, maybe even hate him, and he has started to realize the feeling is somewhat mutual. He is sick of being expected to make love to Beth and no one but Beth. Enough is frickin' enough, for godsake.

Above his desk hang photos of Wright and Pei and Gehry and Julia Morgan, along with posters of Fallingwater and the Louvre pyramid. He stares at them, oddly transfixed, though the photos have hung there for years. He suddenly feels bogus, as if he should instead have a Ringling Brothers poster hanging there, or maybe a poster featuring a third-string rock band or a movie poster of Brando astride a Harley. He might as well have a vulgar velvet painting of a clown, something fit for the "bonus room" in the cheesiest of suburban tract houses. He is irrelevant in his own profession and an outsider in his own life.

His father would have preferred castration to sitting at a desk or gabbling in a classroom or lecture hall, his arms as unmuscled as a girl's. A longshoreman's trade was a masculine undertaking, a job that was vigorous and kinetic.

From one of the desk drawers Slater removes a small, framed black-and-white photo of his parents on their wedding day. Years ago the photo stood on the desktop, but he soon realized that none of his colleagues kept family photos in their offices. Also, the students asked too many questions and Slater grew sick of making the same small talk. Mom and Poppy were married during World War II and wear their uniforms in the photo. Poppy, a curly-haired sailor, is sporting his dress whites, and Mom, a lovely, red-lipped WAVE, wears a dark suit nipped in at the waist, and an unflattering military cap. She always expressed regret about not being married in a white gown and veil, but war was war, she said. At least his parents had not been the sort of dorks who wanted to "renew their vows" twenty years later, aging people donning the youthful attire of dewy brides and grooms. In this instant he recalls something he has not thought about in years: after the war, Mom made David a little suit of clothes out of the fabric from his parents' military uniforms, a child-sized navy blue suit with short pants. Somewhere there is still a photo of Slater in the getup. He can remember being proud of the suit but embarrassed by the headgear: Mom had for some inexplicable reason made a tartan Glengarry cap, trailing ribbon and all, and everyone but David had found the headgear adorable.

He continues scrutinizing his parents' wedding photo. Are there visible signs of something in his father's psyche that would drive Poppy to annihilate himself only months after Mom's death? Or maybe he is searching for clues to what it is about a couple that can bind them together for fifty years.

There is a knock on Slater's office door, followed by a female voice. "Dr. Slater?" The voice is thin and high-register; she's probably an undergrad. At first he does not respond. "Dr. Slater?" she repeats. He calls out for her to come in.

Out of his unconscious rises a random phrase he remembers from long ago—he'll google it later—"swift and secure flight."

Slater sits at a table in Siesta Sancho's with two women from the Wednesday night suicide survivors support group. He and the expat Californian, Holly, and the Oklahoma gal named SueAnn have begun having margaritas weekly after group for a postgame recap. Tonight Slater has declined a cocktail and substituted a club soda with lime, unnerved by the booze fest in L.A. His midsection throbs, but the pressure belt is not visible under his shirt. No one seems to have noticed that his spare tire is gone.

Slater spies a young woman with an iPhone pointed directly at him. He recognizes her as one of his grad students, sitting at the bar along with some other girls. Every now and then, he spots students photographing him about town with their smartphone cameras. Who knew that when he left New York, he would go on to garner paparazzi in Oklahoma, any semblance of privacy kaput? He gives the girl a mock salute and she quickly turns away.

"Sometimes, going to group starts to seem like self-indulgent whining," Slater says.

For a moment neither woman speaks, and Slater hears the steady crunching sound of Holly chewing the ice from her margarita.

"Do you mean me?" SueAnn says, her round little face reddening. "I guess I shouldn't have been complaining about Gilbert again."

Slater feels a pang of regret. Why does he never consider how other people might respond to things he says? "No, no, I didn't mean you, hon. We're always interested in what you have to say."

Holly says, "Dave, is that why you said almost nothing tonight in group—because you didn't want to whine? Or maybe there was something you didn't want to say?"

"Nah, nothing like that," Slater says, telling her he is simply overtired from a trip to California for book research.

SueAnn, who always seems cognizant of uneasiness in others, chooses a topic-changing gambit. "I saw your wife today when I was at work in the store," she tells Slater. "I recognized her from the time I saw you together at the Farmer's Market, but I don't think she recognized me."

Slater had not realized that Beth shopped at the Dollar Thrift-O. Well, who can guess about someone else's life, even their spouse's? He cuts to the chase: "Was she alone?"

SueAnn confirms that Beth was by herself.

"What did she buy?" he asks.

Poor SueAnn actually stutters her answer and seems extremely discomfited; her face again turns a deep red. "I don't know. I wasn't the one who rang her up," she says. "But she's a real pretty lady, very nice looking."

"I cheated on her in L.A.," he announces.

SueAnn's and Holly's faces register shock, and Holly even covers the bottom half of her face with her hands. But this much he knows for sure: they are not even half as surprised as he is. Until the very moment the confession spilled from his mouth, he would have sworn on Poppy's grave he was not going to tell anyone about his misconduct.

"But . . ." SueAnne says, not finishing her thought. She and Holly both wear the bug-eyed, slack-jawed expressions of actors miming surprise on a TV sitcom.

Slater touches the arm of a waiter passing by the table. "I'll have a Rusty Nail, please."

Slater and the women sit in silence. The pressure belt sears his waist like a branding iron.

As he walks from Sancho's to his car, even though his heels are now bandaged, Slater still feels the pain of each step forward and has to suffer the indignity of walking with a stuttering gait like some old gaffer. But in this instant, out of nowhere, the stabbing sensation in his feet calls forth something. Slater is a kid, maybe four or five, and he is limping along with Poppy, the bottoms of his feet radiating pain. He is wearing his brand-new summer sandals, which his mother, with what Slater years later realized was Depression-era mentality, has insisted on buying a size too large in order for him to "grow into them"—a phrase that actually means the shoes will be too large for several months and will then begin to fit properly just as the weather becomes too cold for sandals. The friction of the sandals slipping and sliding and rubbing against his feet has raised hellish blisters.

It's just Davey and Poppy, and they are walking from the green DeSoto across a parking lot that is paved with hot asphalt. They are in Queens, at Rockaway Beach. Where was Mom that day? He cannot now guess why he and his father went to Rockaway on their own. But he does remember the smells, the smell of sand and salt water and sweet taffy and popcorn and Sea and Ski sunscreen—still called "suntan lotion" in those days. God, the sensory montage intoxicates him even in this moment. He begged his father to take him directly to Playland, saving the beach for later, but his father, always mesmerized by the ocean, tugged at his hand. In those days Rockaway was still known as the Irish Riviera, and the surfing culture had not yet sprung up. But Rockaway's Playland was amusement-park heaven to the boy, even more than Coney Island. One of the most calamitous events of Slater's adult life was Playland being torn down in '87 and replaced by houses.

On this particular day at Rockaway, Davey Slater had been able to think only of the carousel and a bag of salted peanuts in a striped paper sack. He envisioned himself astride a huge wooden steed, goading the painted horse with the leather strap and galloping along on the carousel, munching peanuts at the same time. His mouth now waters. But another sensation set in for Davey Slater at that point: he and his father stepped onto the sandy beach, and as he trudged forward, sand bunched in his sandals and settled in lumps that rubbed against the watery blisters on the bottom of his feet. Tears burned his eyes, but he did not want his father to see him crying.

"Never mind, buddy," Poppy told him. "We'll do the beach later—let's schlep over to the rides." His father picked him up and hoisted him to his broad shoulders, rescuing his son's stinging feet from the hot sand. Poppy wore a white cotton T-shirt, smooth and soft under Slater's bare legs. One of Poppy's cartoonishly large forearms bore a garish tattoo featuring a large anchor and the words U.S. Navy—this in the days before tattoos were within the purview of young hipsters but were still somewhat louche emblems of working-class men and GIs. From the T-shirt rose the new-mown-fragrant scent of the Tide detergent in which Mom washed the family's clothing. Being astride his strong father's powerful longshoreman's shoulders was even more thrilling than riding a carousel horse, and Slater was infused with a nearly beatific joy.

Two smells of that instant now enter Slater's nose again, not remembered but actually present—the primary scents of everyone's father in the fifties, Prell shampoo and Old Spice.

He slogs forward, his feet and midsection blowtorching his body, heading toward his car, which will take him to his house, where he will have to talk with Beth. Another of the slogans Poppy sometimes repeated was that people never lie so much as after a hunt or before a war.

Slater has tried for more than a year to tamp down thoughts of his father. He knows that memory is the ultimate gill net, ready to snare you and yank you away from your source of air. But lately he has been slipping down, sinking into that opal-dark pool. He does not seem to be able to remember *himself* in a very good light. What floats up is the recollection of the time he called his father an asshole, or the time when he was fifteen and took money out of his mother's pocketbook.

Limping, Slater makes his way toward his Solstice, which is parked in the front of the Sancho's lot. The neon sign on the front of the seafood restaurant across the street from Siesta Sancho's looks as if it hovers near the roof of his car. The blue neon fish swimming across the facade of Cap'n Cabral's seems to swim along Slater's car, the illusion simply a matter of perspective. In the days when David and his father used to fish at Breezy Point, Poppy had explained to him that when fish are taken out of water, they suffocate not because they cannot breathe the oxygen available in the air but because their gill arches collapse and there is not enough surface area for diffusion to take place; the breaking down is a fundamental principle of engineering. The luminous fish swims out of Slater's sight.

DROP ZONE

When cold, we gather 'round the blazing fire;
When hot, we sit on the bank of the mountain
stream in the bamboo grove

The Zenrin Kushu

Only the ugly survive. As she waters the silvery-purple coleus in the living room, Holly mentally kisses the plant goodbye. Though it looks fine now, it cannot possibly live. The plants that thrive are the unsightly ones, spindly viny plants or those with thick and rubbery leaves.

Food can fake you out, too: attractive food tastes bad and ugly food tastes good, as if the universe has a droll sense of humor. When she was first married, she brought home some produce from the supermarket, telling her husband, "Look at this gorgeous head of lettuce!" Theo laughingly informed her that the lettuce was actually cabbage.

Holly has read that Marilyn Monroe chose food for its appearance, too. When Monroe was still Norma Jean and newly married, she had served her husband a dinner of nothing but carrots and peas on a plate.

When he stared at the plate and then at her, she told him she thought the orange and green looked pretty together.

The palmlike plant Holly paid big bucks for has lost all its bottom leaves, and the top fronds are curled and brownish. She dumps the dying plant into the garbage and takes the empty pot to the storage cabinet in the laundry room. When she opens the cabinet door, she sees it: a smaller pot, hand-thrown, with a green cactus painted on the front. Reed threw the pot in a ceramics class he took when they were still living in La Jolla. How odd that she has not looked inside this cabinet in an entire year. Oh, merde, her knees are actually jellying. She learned long before that most of the grief clichés are entirely true. Yeah, you go through the denial, the rage, the watered-down acceptance—you wear the dead person's sweaters or robe, blah blah—it's all true. But weird stuff happens, too, things you never dreamed of. Just when the year-mark has passed and you think you have begun to recover, think you might be ready to move on, you see him in the supermarket weighing cantaloupe: Reed, not a dead man's ashes in an engraved urn in the Calabasas cemetery chosen by his parents, but a vibrant, young, alive man buying produce at the grocery. Then, when he turns his head, of course he is not Reed after all.

She does not wish to think about the other thing—the thing she had forgotten about until one Sunday afternoon when she watched a video about the singer Leonard Cohen. Cohen lost his father when he was nine years old and subsequently created his own private grief ritual that he performed in secret. Cohen reported that he took one of his deceased father's bow ties, which still smelled of his father's after-shave, and slit open a portion of the fabric. He wrote a note to his dead father, telling him everything he wished he had said before his father died, folded up the note, and stuffed it into the bow tie. The young Cohen then slipped outside and buried the tie and the note in the garden, his own secret monument. Holly had cried out when she heard Cohen share this story, scaring Teddy, who came running into the room where she was watching the video. Poor Teddy—he had been through enough, losing his quasi-stepfather and having a mother half crazy with grief. She told her son she had simply had a sneezing fit.

But what she had remembered in that instant was that she had done something. Something that might have been touching if a child had done it, but in an adult was creepy and unwell. She had written a note to the dead Reed, begging him to come back to her and saying she would wait for him. She slipped the note inside Rumi's *Book of Love: Poems of Ecstasy and Longing*, a volume given to her by Reed, with an inscription in Reed's own hand. She is well enough now, more than a year later, not to allow herself to take the book from the bottom drawer of the night table and look at her note to Reed. And Reed has *not* come back, has he?

Instead there is the man on the online dating site, Reed's doppelgänger, originally calling himself Waiting4U. The first time she saw the man's photo, she was certain he was actually Reed, still alive after all. After a few brief e-mail exchanges, he has revealed his actual name is Jeremiah.

While for the most part Jeremiah can spell, and though he has never written in his e-mails anything vulgar, overtly stupid, or untoward, what is also true is that he is not exactly within her usual dating pool. *Dating pool*—who is she kidding even to think in such terms? She has never dated much; she met Reed only weeks after leaving her husband, and she had been with Reed five years at the time he shot himself. What she really means is that in the amorphous, primarily imagined world of men she might be willing to kiss, none of these are men with less education than she has or who are less urbane than Reed. The Internet look-alike works as a tree surgeon, which does call forth a few semi-sexy images. And also in Jeremiah's favor, he has not asked to telephone or meet her for coffee yet. He seems astute enough to sense she wants nothing beyond e-mail, at least for now. Or maybe that's all he wants, too.

This morning Holly drove Teddy to a school pal's house across town for a play date, and her bookstore is closed on Sundays. Maybe before she immerses herself in e-Luv, she ought to have a light lunch and a glass of Shiraz. She was never one to drink wine with lunch, or even beer before five p.m., but lots of things have changed since Reed's death. If she is honest with herself, she has become a lousy mother and an occasional tippler, as well as being chronically depressed. Were it not for Teddy, the image of herself in the gutter would not be difficult to conjure.

She finds a can of sardines in the kitchen cupboard, stacks some Wasa crackers on a plate, and uncorks what is left of last night's bottle of wine. She lowers the can of sardines into the sink so she can drain off the oil.

She carefully rolls back the key on the can, then lifts it to pull away from the tin. You would think they could have developed a more user-friendly way to open a can by now.

She sees the wound before she feels it: a bright stream of blood flows from her wrist where the lid has snapped sharply backward and cut her. Even before a glass of wine—this is hilarious—she has inadvertently slashed her wrist with a sardine can and is bleeding profusely.

She binds up her wrist with a dish towel, but when the towel is nearly completely red, she succumbs to panic. What if the tin hit an artery and she bleeds out right here on the less-than-immaculate kitchen floor, next to some unwashed dishes and a can full of oil and fish? *What a dingy way to die.* But she comes to her senses and applies firmer pressure to the wrist.

Holly has worn a long-sleeved blouse to the weekly meeting of the suicide survivors, although the room in the church hall is chronically overly warm. Her left wrist beneath her sleeve is wrapped several times over with gauze and tape, the definitive dressing for her slash wound. In her kitchen on Sunday, she had to apply pressure to the wound for some minutes before the bleeding let up, and she has bandaged and re-bandaged her wrist daily as the blood resumed seeping. She has always been a bleeder, her skin as thin as a promise.

Dave has been talking about some problems with one of his students, but suddenly he sits stock still and says, "What's that?" He points with an alarmed expression to her sleeve.

When she looks down, she sees dots of blood speckling the cuff of her white blouse. "It's nothing," she assures the group. "I accidentally cut my wrist when I was opening some sardines." She laughs nervously, the only sound in the room for some moments.

Finally Dave says, "Are you sure the suicide spell isn't kicking in, hon?"

Holly, feeling she is being accused, tells him not to be silly, it was just a simple kitchen accident.

Dr. Jane says, "Someone once said there are no accidents." She winks.

Holly observes that everyone in the circle is looking sorrowfully at her. Clearly they all think she has made an attempt, or at least a dramatic gesture that could be a cry for help. Well, screw it. Dr. Jane is liable to go Freudian on her no matter what Holly might say, and as for Dave and SueAnn, she can clear things up with them when they have their customary margaritas at Siesta Sancho's after group tonight.

While SueAnn tells the group about the latest dustup between her and her husband—her dead child's father—Holly wonders if she should tell the group about the new book she just ordered for the self-help section of her bookstore. *Fall Out of Love: Lose That Baggage* seems guaranteed to garner a few buyers, so Holly ordered three copies and is waiting to see how the book sells. Being in love with a dead man is something Dr. Jane has repeatedly pointed out is supremely unhealthy as well as technically not possible, so it follows that Holly should have no reason to read such a book.

But she can be in love with a dead man, is the problem.

Holly takes Teddy to school, then goes back home to spend some alone time reading *Fall Out of Love: Lose That Baggage*. The first thing she encounters in chapter 1 is a list of "candidates for healing." Among these candidates are the woman who is obsessed with a married man, the woman madly in love with someone who does not return her feelings, the woman in love with a man young enough to be her son, the woman in love with a man who is "draining" her emotionally and financially. Maybe the last one might have been Holly when Reed was alive.

The author, a psychologist, suggests that every time the reader begins to think of the object of desire, she is to replace the incoming thought about the loved one with an extremely negative image.

"Envisioning the object of desire in such a negative manner can be scary at first," claims the author. Holly dislikes the word "scary," a babyish term of which the therapeutic community these days, including Dr. Jane, seems inordinately fond. She urges herself to read on, nonetheless. The author shares with her readers some of the negative images her clients have conjured to ban any romantic thoughts of their loved ones: envisioning him picking his nose; imagining him with missing teeth and shriveled genitals, walking down the street nude, mumbling to himself; seeing him with greenish pig vomit smeared all over him.

Oh, darling Reed, beautiful Reed, I can't do that to you, Holly thinks. I might be willing to fall out of love with you, but I can't defile your memory.

She closes the book. The back cover features a blurb that claims the book is a "masterpiece of clarity, a simple, logical process for breaking the bonds of memories that maim." She hears the soft, mellow ringing of the fake wind chimes she keeps on the bedroom bureau top. She and Reed were shopping once in Target and kept hearing the mellifluous and soothing tinkling of what sounded like wind chimes. Arm in arm, they had followed the sound, zigzagging the aisles, tracking the source as if it were the Holy Grail. And suddenly there it was, perched on top of a display tower at the end of one aisle in the housewares section: an indoor wind chime, its melodious knelling occurring at regular intervals.

"It's oddly relaxing," Reed said.

They watched as every few seconds a timed puff of air rose from the battery-operated base and ruffled the tubular bells, initiating a soft, air-blown ringing sound. "Gotta love it," Reed said, and picked up one of the boxed devices and placed it atop the other items he carried in one of the store's small red baskets.

The chimes ended up in their bedroom, and now she cannot hear the tinkly jingle-jangle without having vivid flashbacks to love scenes between her and Reed. Scientists have documented the fact that memory and taste are linked in the brain, and that by stimulating a memory-storing segment of the brain, a person will potently smell something that is not actually present in the room. But for her, the tinkling sound is the source of those Proustian moments. She is aroused now, simmering beneath her clothing, and rushes to the bedroom, ashamed, to press the button that switches off the chimes.

Her laptop rests on the kitchen table, and she has been scrolling through the e-Luv messages while Teddy stands at the stove. Jeremiah wants to meet her.

"Some man wants to take me on a date," she tells Teddy.

Teddy's back is to her as he stirs oatmeal. When he visited his father during the summer, Theo taught him how to cook breakfast.

"Who *is* the man?" Teddy says.

She tells him the guy is someone she met through a dating service. The sound of a spoon scraping a pan is for a few moments the only noise in the room. Then, Teddy says with clear annoyance, "Why doesn't he have a wife? There must be something wrong with him."

Holly laughs. "I'm not married, either. Does that mean there's something wrong with me, too?"

"You can't help it if Reed did what he did," Teddy says as he ladles oatmeal into two bowls. "He did a bad thing—that's why you're not married."

She says nothing, glad he does not broach the subject of her going back to Theo, which might be what Teddy actually wants. Nor does she tell him Jeremiah's wife died. Teddy does not need any further grisly information.

"He could be a sereo killer," Teddy says, placing a bowl before her.

She says she is sure the guy's not a serial killer, though maybe she is not as certain as she hopes she sounds.

"Do you notice something?" Teddy says.

She looks up from the screen, then follows Teddy's glance downward to her cereal bowl. Teddy has fashioned a smiley face on her oatmeal. Raisins form eyes and a nose, and for the smiling mouth he has smeared some strawberry jam in an upward curving line. She swallows the catch in her throat and tells him he is the sweetest son, ever. She has not exactly believed in God for quite some time, but there is no doubt her child was sent Express Mail straight from the Big Kahuna.

She closes the cover of the laptop and pushes the computer aside so she can eat breakfast. When she unfolds the newspaper, she discovers a peculiar story on the second page. It seems a young man, a skydiving student, was taking his maiden voyage, a piggyback jump with his instructor, a middle-aged man. A few seconds after they jumped from the plane, the instructor pulled the rip cord, then shouted over the wind into the novice's ear, "Welcome to my world!" When the student called back a question, he was met with silence. Soon realizing the man on his back was unconscious, the student had the presence of mind to correctly position his body as they approached the drop zone, and he managed to make a safe landing. The older man was unstrapped from his back, stone dead, and taken away in a body bag.

Teddy peruses the comics page while Holly sips her coffee. She closes her eyes, and shimmering there in the darkness behind her eyelids is the image: a man leaping from a plane, flying free, the blazes of noon enfolding him and wind hissing in his ears, a dead man strapped to his back.

When she reopens the laptop, she discovers a new message from Jeremiah. "The jig's up," she says to herself.

Teddy asks her what she means, and she tells him, "I mean I have to 'fish or cut bait.' I either meet this Jeremiah guy or let him go—my choice."

"My choice is no," her son says. He does not look at her but continues examining the comics page of the *Tulsa World*.

She says nothing, but she is fully aware that, more often than not, Teddy is correct about things, wise beyond his years—even wise beyond hers. He was crazy about Reed in a manner that was very similar to her own besottedness: dazzled, but not blind to Reed's not-inconsequential shortcomings. Once, when Teddy was only six, he said to Holly, "Reed's messed up—he doesn't *want* to be happy." She was astonished by the accuracy of her child's observation. Reed was edgy when things were going well; he gravitated toward calamity, toward what Yeats called "fabulous, formless darkness." She guesses that being a compulsive gambler served Reed's crimped psyche very well. She has little doubt that plenty of his fellow devotees of online poker and smoky Indian-reservation casinos were there for the same reason Reed had actually been: to lose.

Holly has just rung up still another copy of *The Purpose Driven Life*. Funny the way situations work out: if she had her druthers, such a book would not smell up her bookstore, but this very book has turned out to be the bread and butter of H. Hemenway, Booksellers. Cadon, her part-time clerk, is listlessly stocking the shelves. She can sense that before too long he will resign and she will have to train someone new. Maybe she can poach someone from the bookstore at the university, offering a higher salary than the school can pay. Not that she can afford to pay much, either. She knows it is just a matter of time—and not all that much time—before her shaky business goes completely belly-up. If she were at the top of her game, she would be aggressively devising a Plan B rather than playing the denial card. The fact is, even if she stripped the shop of real literature and turned the place into a Christian bookstore, she would still end up going broke before too long. Books themselves are sliding into society's dumper. She will burn the place to the ground before she will have anything whatever to do with electronic reading devices like Kindle. Not only is she brick and mortar, she will forever be paper and ink.

The bell over the door tinkles. She looks toward Cadon, but he pretends not to have heard, so she walks toward the front of the store herself, preparing to offer the default greeting.

As the man steps across the threshold, he raises his chin and looks her full in the face. She momentarily teeters on a fulcrum between instant recognition and immediate rejection: It's Reed / He's not Reed / He's Jeremiah / Oh crap. Within two seconds she has experienced shock, bliss, disappointment, and resignation, and now stands mute, waiting to see what Jeremiah will say.

"Holly?"

Jeremiah offers his hand and she reaches out to shake it and says, "How do you do," with what she can tell is a stiff, formal tone. In the flesh, his resemblance to Reed is not pronounced, though he has the same unusual dark red hair and a similarly shaped jaw. "I'm Holly," she says, then laughs nervously. Of course he already knows who she is; he just called her by name.

"I'm Jeremiah," he responds. "I hope y'all don't mind my coming in."

He seems too genuine and even artlessly sweet for her to consider him a stalker. He is a handsome man, too. But then he smiles. This otherwise nice-looking online suitor not only has teeth that are worse than any Irishman's, there is actually a gap where a tooth is missing. Trying not to betray her shock, she says something noncommittal and walks toward the coffee machine at the back of the shop, motioning him to follow. Her heart beats wildly, and she is hyper-aware of Cadon drawing a bead on them. The most absurd thing is that in this moment all she can think of is a rude joke she heard a disc jockey make on the radio: "The stadium in Oklahoma City was filled with fifty thousand people, which added up to a hundred thousand teeth." She does not wish to be a snob, but until she came to Oklahoma, she had never before seen a person with missing teeth, except for carneys at the California State Fair.

She offers Jeremiah coffee, and when he accepts, she pours mugs for them both. He is chattering a bit nervously, probably wondering if maybe he should not have come into the shop. She feels bad for him, poor guy. He says something about remembering she said she owned a bookstore, and when he googled the words "Holly" and "Hope Springs," up had popped the website of H. Hemenway, Booksellers. Taking the mug of coffee from her, Jeremiah walks beside her to the small tables at the back of the store but stops and points to one of the top shelves on the store's perimeter.

"Oh, my favorite book," he says, and for an instant she feels a frisson of hope, but he has indicated Rick Warren's book. *The Purpose Driven Life*," he says, clearly proud of his erudition. Evidently he does not recall that he listed this book as his favorite within his e-Luv profile, but she does not say anything about this. At least he reads; cut the man a break. "I really like Michael Crichton, too," he says.

She nods. She knows that Crichton writes page-turners—and that he's been married five times and is a vocal denier of climate change. But forget Jeremiah's literary tastes and his teeth and for godsake try to be kind for a change. Who cares if Cadon is staring at them with what Holly has come to think of as his little-grad-student smirk. He's a lazy sod in any case and Jeremiah is, for all Cadon knows, a paying customer who should be treated as such. "Were you looking for a particular book today?"

"Well, I was looking for something inspirational, but maybe something by Crichton, too." She tells him he might be interested in Kubler-Ross, and asks if he has ever read Scott Turow. She will worry later about how to let him down gently as a suitor. As for Cadon, maybe she will fire him before he can quit. Just last week she saw him in a restaurant wearing a red beret; who is he to sneer at Jeremiah?

When she and Jeremiah walk together to the Self-Help section, somehow she finds herself looking down at his shoes. The shoes. She recognizes them immediately, an uncommon style of Nike she has never seen anyone but Reed wear. She self-corrects: anyone but Reed *buy*, as the shoes were never worn after Reed purchased them. The shoes are a hybrid of bohemian and thug, black-on-black-on-black, even the swoosh black. The recollection of throwing the box of brand-new shoes into the Rubbermaid trash can behind her house is as vivid as if she had done it an hour ago. She could smell the new-shoe smell when she discarded the box, heaving it on top of some chicken bones and a Rice Dream carton. Air Monarch III was printed on the shoe box.

This is the worst part: lying in bed without Reed next to her. After his death, she moved the bedroom furniture to what was formerly the study and vice versa, but decamping from their former bedroom has not helped. The new mattress has not helped, either, nor have the new bed linens, bedding that mercifully does not smell like Reed. No matter how many times she washed their old quilt and blanket, she swore she could still detect Reed's heady scent, so finally she discarded them and bought new bedding from Bed Bath & Beyond. It's the "beyond" that has her in its narcotic-like spell of remembrance.

Her initial attraction to Reed had been based on his intelligence and wit and, admittedly, his good looks. But then sex entered the picture and everything careered out of bounds. She had fallen into a raptured state of eros, plummeting into the secret zone of just the two of them like Alice down the rabbit hole. And, yes, it had been transcendent—even Tantric. Dr. Jane has dismissed the heat between Reed and her as "erotic enmeshment." They had not really come up for air until the week before Reed shot himself. That week, they had not even touched each other. She could count on the fingers of one hand how many times she and Reed had been in bed together without making love. But the week before he died, Reed sat in front of the television every evening with the sound off, smoking. Already envisioning himself on the other side, though she had not realized it.

She is not at all certain that Reed actually intended buying shoes only as a ruse. Maybe he just was not sure, four days before he shot himself, that he was really going to take his own life; maybe he was vacillating. He had driven to Dillard's and bought the expensive new pair of black Nikes, showing the shoes to her and Teddy before placing them back in the box and into the closet, where they remained until after he killed himself.

Who buys pricey new shoes right before he kills himself? He had not even worn the footwear that awful day—it's not as if he had wanted his body taken away with unsullied Nikes on his feet

Fall Out of Love is not the first pop psychology self-help book Holly ever read. Once, she read a book about "self-love," a book she bought accidentally. She had assumed the book was about self-esteem, of which she had been devoid at the time she purchased the book, just after she and Theo broke up. But it turned out the book was actually about onanism, that kind of self-love. At first she had slammed the cover shut, embarrassed. But she was too sheepish to return the book to the store where she bought it and so ended up reading the thing. The author claimed that women's sexual fantasies differed from men's in several ways, one of which was this: women fantasized only about acts in which they already engaged, whereas men's fantasies roamed to uncharted territory. The claim offended Holly at the time. She still believed then that men and women were not only equal but the same, essentially interchangeable, save for their differing genitalia. She had bought Teddy both trucks and dolls when he was a baby, not wishing to imprint him with gender expectations. To her surprise, Teddy never once looked at the dolls, but he played with the trucks until the wheels fell off. And while neither she nor Theo ever allowed toy guns, she has been dismayed to see that Teddy fashions guns out of everything from pencils to empty cardboard toilet paper rollers.

And wasn't that pop psychology guy correct, after all? Has she ever had a sexual fantasy about anything other than being with a current or past lover? Trying to imagine making love even with Johnny Depp is a failed enterprise. Five seconds into the fantasy, Reed's slender body and exotic angular face will superimpose themselves over those of Depp, and only then will she sink into that zone of mindless heat and of deliverance.

Alone now in Reed's and her bed, Teddy asleep down the hall in his own bed, she tries to avoid going to Reed in the dark of the room, tries not to touch herself, and when she touches herself anyway, she tries the bad-fantasy exercise suggested in *Fall Out of Love*.

Instead of giving in to the images of alive-Reed, she replaces him with an unpleasant Reed avatar, one who is hairy where he should be smooth and bald where he should have hair. A Reed whose breath is not minty/airy but fetid. A Reed who cannot make her writhe and cry out and weep and even nearly black out: *la petite mort*. An inept Reed. But the ploy does not work. Once again an image of the real Reed, deadly sexy and succulent and irreplaceable, overpowers the fabricated unsavory image, and again she is with Reed in the night.

When she wakes, at first Holly thinks morning has arrived and she needs to get up and go to work in the store. But the room is dark, and from the partially opened bedroom window she hears women shouting, accompanied by the sounds of a scuffle. "Do you know what you've fucking done?" one of the women screams, and Holly hears a volley of slapping sounds, followed by cries and curses from two different female voices. The noise seems to originate from the vicinity of the next-door neighbors' front porch. She sits up in bed, then remembers there had been a loud party going on next door, and that Teddy had wakened about midnight and called out to her from his bedroom down the hall. She had been propped up in bed watching a DVD of *Blue Velvet*—a bad idea in any case, as the song "In Dreams" brings back excruciating memories of the days following Reed's death. A glass of chocolate milk and a few soothing words had put Teddy back to sleep, but she had been irritated when she turned out her own bedroom light and tried to fall asleep. The sounds of loud hip-hop music, drunken laughter, and the repeated slamming of car doors went on for some time before she managed to doze off.

The illuminated numerals on the alarm clock indicate the time is now 3:00 a.m. Damn—the neighbors had seemed normal enough, until tonight.

"You piece of shit! Fuck you!" a woman shouts, and Holly hears the sound of slaps and some screams. "Get out! Get the hell out!"

She gets out of bed and peers through the shutters, but the side hedge blocks her view. One of the women is now sobbing as the scuffling sounds continue. Again and again someone shouts, "You fucking bitch! You fucking bitch! Do . . . you . . . realize . . . what . . . you've . . . *done?*"

Holly shuts the window and turns on the television to mask the sound entirely. A shouting man with a beard hawks a spot-removal product, but she does not bother to change the channel. She switches on the air chime machine for its soothing effect.

There is no valid reason to do what she does now. But she finds herself opening the bottom drawer of the bedside table and pulling out the old leather-bound volume of Rumi, the one in which Reed had written on the title page.

When she opens the front cover, the sight of Reed's haphazard handwriting jolts her to the core, and for an instant she reels backward, woozy as if she had just inhaled gasoline fumes. She knows in this instant that graphology is indeed an exact science: Reed's handwriting is so manifestative of his personality, his *essence*, that it seems as if she has looked at a photo of him or heard his voice. She has closed the cover without meaning to, so she opens the book again, more slowly to avoid a second profound shock to her senses.

> *"You're water. We're the millstone*
> *You're wind. We're dust blown up into shapes."*
> *I love you into eternity,* *
> *Yours, Reed*

At the bottom of the page, Reed referenced the asterisk by writing "Or at least until I'm 39." Pure Reed—just like the "Goodbye, cruel world" in his suicide note. Always with Reed there was the one-two punch: fervor countered by sardonic humor. The irony is that she doubts very much that Reed realized when he scribbled the coda to Rumi's verse that he in fact would not make it to thirty-nine.

Holly turns to the page where she tucked the note she wrote to Reed just after his death but spares herself the added pain of unfolding the note and reading it. She raises the folded sheet of paper to her nose and breathes in the scent. The paper inexplicably carries the bouquet of cardamom and clove, summoning images of Reed, his face candlelit, across from her at their favorite Indian restaurant.

When she was in her twenties, Holly had worked her way through reading the Russians. She started with Tolstoy, moved on to Turgenev and Gogol and Chekhov and Lermontov, segueing into the divine, incomparable Dostoyevsky. But the one thing that cropped up in the works of each author was what was termed "brain fever." The designation covered everything from tuberculosis to puerperal fever to a mild nervous condition to a full psychotic break. Brain fever was cited as the cause or result of everything from depression to death. Often a jilted lover or a widowed woman would immediately fall into bed suffering from brain fever.

If only we could have brain fever now, Holly wishes. Why couldn't I have just signed out for a few months with brain fever after I discovered Reed with his face blown nearly off? Maybe the brain fever could have been timed well enough so that it struck me down before I found myself crawling down the hall, away from Reed's body and to the telephone, as if the EMT people could arrive and put Reed's skull back together. But two really necessary phenomena did not make it to the twenty-first century: brain fever and expedient syncope. Maybe if we still wore whalebone corsets and still took paregoric during menses, we might be able to faint dead away every time something terrible happened. But no, women are fit and healthy now, forced to be fully awake and aware, obliged to endure every unbearable moment.

Holly slides the note back into the book and returns the Rumi to the drawer. At least she no longer writes letters to the dead. She even understands now why she composed the brainsick plea to the deceased Reed in the first place. During their grief support meetings, garrulous Dave sometimes quotes his Russian grandmother. Last week's granny maxim was "Hope is a fool's mother, but the only mother we have."

After she lies back down and pulls up the blankets, Holly mutes the television's audio. The huckster selling stain removers has been replaced by a commercial for oatmeal. She has never seen this particular ad before, and in the dark of her bedroom the soundless image illuminating the screen arrests her attention. A man wearing a dress shirt and necktie stands poised for flight. On his back he wears a twin pack of cylindrical oatmeal boxes, which together look like a Jetpack, the mechanism that, when strapped to one's back, allows one to actually fly. How many times, sleeping in this very room, has she had dreams of flying, rising up and away, above all the grit and hurly-burly of earth and soaring free?

Once she saw a Jetpack demo on the Internet, a video clip of a man flying. His Jetpack emitted a loud, dissonant sound, more like Holly's mother's old Kirby vacuum cleaner than like an airplane. As the man flew, two attendants ran along, below and to the side of the flying man, ready to catch him if he fell.

Now the oatmeal man is aloft, lifted into the air and gliding in a blue sky, briefcase bobbing in the wind, farther and farther above roads and buildings, his arms at his sides like gull wings. He ascends.

BURGLAR

It is easier for a father to have children
than for children to have a father.

POPE JOHN XXIII

"No foul play is suspected," the cable news guy says. Slater looks up from
where he is sitting on the sofa with a stack of exams turned in by the students in his Theory of Architecture seminar. Funny how a phrase such as
"no foul play suspected" can be clichéd and yet at the same time have the
power to set off a Pavlovian response. He feels a spritz of cold sweat beneath his shirt as his father comes to mind. In the case of Poppy's suicide
last year, Slater knew foul play had in fact been suspected by the cops. His
father had set up the Salvadoran housekeeper, telling her he was going
out of town and asking her to come in and feed the dog while he was away.
When she entered the house to feed Poppy's elderly borzoi, the unfortunate woman found her employer in bed ashen and deceased, with a bottle
of Captain Morgan and an empty prescription bottle on the nightstand.
The cops then roped the porch with yellow crime-scene tape and ques-
tioned her for some time. He guesses he should feel grateful that Poppy

arranged things so none of his children would find the corpse, but there is something unsavory about sticking a domestic worker with such a task. Another hackneyed expression comes to mind: "Not in my job description."

His attention drifts back to the TV, where the news guy elaborates on the no-foul-play story at hand. The item turns out to be one of those Ripley's-type tales, freakishly unlikely. Some guy in South Carolina had received a heart transplant several years before and bizarrely enough ended up marrying the widow of his own heart donor. But the story had not ended there. Now, six years later, he has been found dead with what appears to be a self-inflicted shotgun wound, which as it happens is exactly the way the donor himself had died.

It enters Slater's mind that maybe the widow shot both men, but apparently the cops have ruled out that possibility. Could there really be something uncanny about the donor heart? Could an organ—other than the one below the waist—actually cause one man after another to fall in love with the very same woman and then to raise a gun to his head, too? The story momentarily rattles him. But probably the twice-widowed woman drove both husbands to suicide; probably the transplanted heart had nothing to do with the issue.

Now the local news has replaced the national stuff, and on the screen is a haggard-looking woman being interviewed in the front yard of her home. Standing by the chain link fence is an interviewer from one of the Tulsa stations, a reporter wearing a flowered dress of the sort favored by Oklahoma women. The interviewee herself wears a pair of baggy trousers, topped by a maroon Sooners hoodie. She explains in what used to be termed a "whiskey voice," but from the looks of her deeply furrowed face is more likely a voice ravaged by decades of tobacco use, that sometime during the night, someone had stolen her statue of Jesus from this very lawn. She points to a spot in the center of the yard and elaborates.

"He was rot here," she says, "rot in the middle of my yard, the sacred heart a Jesus."

The reporter in the country-cousin dress turns somberly to the camera and informs the audience, "The theft of the statue of Jesus occurred sometime last night. It's hard to *imagine* who would do something like this." She offers a dismayed little head shake.

"Are we gonna let the Debil win?" the complainant says. "Cuz that's what's happenin'."

Beth comes out of the kitchen carrying two glasses of wine. "I think it's the cocktail hour, Dave," she says, eyeing the stack of student papers until Slater sets them aside. "What's *new* on the news?" She hands him a glass.

"The Devil stole Jesus," he says, but keeps his tone nonjudgmental. He has never cared to be one of those like Woody Allen who mock other people's religions. He has no ax to grind against Jesus, even if Jesus-culture is tacky, nor does he make Easter egg jokes, as Allen often did back in his high-visibility days before Soon Yi. Slater says nothing to Beth about the report of the telltale heart that caused men to shoot themselves. He takes a swig of what tastes like Merlot.

Beth leans over to place coasters on the coffee table, and Slater has a close-up view of the backs of her thighs. He wishes he were a bigger person, a more loyal spouse, and that the sight of her cellulite did not impact him negatively. But Slater has begun to discover that he is not a big person, not the man he always intended to be. He has become a clenched-up semi-bitter guy who is often shocked to catch sight of his pinched, unhappy face as he passes a mirror or reflective surface. But Beth had never in their married life worn shorts when they still lived in New York. The women in Hope Springs, though, think nothing of wearing shorts everywhere they go, about seven months out of the year, and Beth has jumped onto that bandwagon. Of course, she's an educated person, so she does not fall for the sucker-bait ads for creams or pills that are supposed to eradicate cellulite. She is aware that those dimples might as well be part of her DNA now, and that they'll be with her in her casket someday.

When he was a freshman at Columbia and still a virgin, he had found himself obsessed with the issue of virginity, wishing his own would disappear and imagining that he was the last male virgin over the age of twelve. He sat in many a seminar or studio session on campus paying little attention to the work at hand, staring at the other students in the room and trying to imagine whether they had sex or not. The preoccupation vexed him like a hair shirt until Homecoming Weekend when Cheryl Bernstein came through for him. Now he finds this sort of OCD thinking has returned, as he stares at every woman he meets, wondering if the backs of her legs are smooth or puckered. He has discovered himself in some unseemly moments trying to catch glimpses of Dr. Jane's thighs when she crosses her legs in her short, flouncy skirts while she facilitates the suicide survivors group meetings on Wednesday evenings.

Beth's voice thrums along with the television; she is making a running commentary on the annoying number of commercials that clog the networks these days, but Slater cannot divorce himself from the story about the guy who shot himself, the guy with the donated heart. And what was it in Slater's father's heart that allowed him to take his life—who could ever know that? Slater remembers a weird factoid from a marine biology course he took long ago at Columbia. The hagfish, which is not exactly a fish but an elongated eel-like creature, has two brains and four hearts. The organism is so flexible it can tie itself in knots.

"Did you ever notice," Beth says, "that when the drug commercials are forced to list the side effects, they do so in a cheery little upbeat singsong voice?"

Slater shrugs.

Beth mimics the commercial being aired: "May cause blindness!" she says in a buoyant tone, "paralysis or cancer!" She flashes an outlandish rictus of a smile, mocking the toothy grin of the actress enumerating the different ways a medication can maim the patient, and Slater has to laugh. Beth, a theater major in college, has always been a talented mimic.

Slater does not recall anything further about the hagfish, though he finds himself wondering how many reproductive organs the critters might have. With all those hearts and brains, does it also need multiple sets of genitalia? How cool would it be to have two schlongs on hand, or maybe a penis and a vagina both, so you never had to worry about a partner. He had taken an undergrad lit seminar, too, as an elective, and there was a Hemingway story in which the young male protagonist looked longingly at women but made no attempt to meet them. The story said the youth dimly desired a girl but did not want to have to work to get her. What he wanted was a "life without consequences."

One day when he was five years old, Slater and two of his neighborhood pals had been playing inside his parents' car. More accurately, the shiny black Plymouth with whitewall tires was his father's car; few women had drivers' licenses in the 1950s. Nearly every family owned only one car, and the man did the driving. Times were different then, as if in a different universe on another plane somewhere. In Flatbush in those days, little kids walked to school without escort, frolicked unchaperoned on playgrounds, rode bikes everywhere, alone or with their chums, played out in the street and inside cars. What they were not allowed to do was listen to the radio when sitting inside their fathers' autos. "You'll wear down the battery!" was the universal parental complaint in Slater's neighborhood. On the day he is recalling, Jeffie Rabinowitz and Barbara Zuchelli had been his playmates, Barbara sitting in the backseat and Jeffie manning the radio as Slater sat in the driver's seat twisting the steering wheel from side to side and making acceleration and braking sounds with his mouth. Jeffie left the radio tuned to a station playing Cliffie Stone's "Silver Stars, Purple Sage." Slater has no idea why cowboy songs were so popular in the 1950s, but there was a whole Western vibe going on then in both music and film. And when the family went out to Playland at the beach, there was a vending machine called Allstar Cowboys where one could slip coins into a slot and choose cowboy cards, just as the adults chose packs of cigarettes from nearly identical machines. Slater had purchased stacks of the cards, and before he went off to Columbia, he discovered in his childhood bureau cards including Bill Elliott as Red Ryder and Robert "Bobby" Blake as Little Beaver; that one is funny now.

"Jeez Louise—your dad's a crook!" Jeffie had opened the glove box and begun rummaging inside with an astonished look on his plump face.

Slater had said, "No, he's not," even before he knew why Rabinowitz made such an accusation.

Rabinowitz gingerly pulled a knife from the glove box and unsheathed it, clutching it in one hand and staring at it as if it were a Tommy gun. "Look at this thing!" he said. "It's gigantic."

"Put it back," Slater said, feeling a hot burning behind his eyes and even in his groin. When Rabinowitz did not re-sheath the knife, Slater repeated more loudly, "Put it back." He added, "And turn off the radio, you'll wear down the battery." He heard Barbara gasp when she saw the knife, and knew she would go home and blab to her parents and her nine siblings. He had heard his father tell his mother that the Zuchellis had so many kids because they were papists, but when Slater asked what that meant, his parents would not say. Slater and his friends left the car, the mood spoiled, and Rabinowitz and Barbara both went home. Slater went inside the house, by then weeping like a wound.

"What's wrong, Davey?" his mother had asked. "Did you skin your knee?"

At first Slater had not wanted to answer his mother, but when she prompted him, he blurted, "Daddy's a burglar."

Mom had first laughed, then asked him why he would think such a thing. He explained he had discovered a knife in the glove box of the car, not mentioning Rabinowitz or the radio.

"Oh, honey, that's a hunting knife," his mother said and put her arm around him. Slater can still feel the relief that surged through him that day, Poppy in an instant transformed from a potential knifer and robber back to his strong, worthy father, a former football player and a navy veteran, a longshoreman who marched proudly with his union brothers in parades.

Just before Slater and Beth were married, lying in bed one long, lazy morning, he had told Beth the anecdote from his childhood about suspecting his father was a "burglar."

"It was just a hunting knife," Slater told her, laughingly ruefully.

Beth had squinted and pressed her lips together, saying nothing at first. Finally she said, "I never thought of your father as a hunter."

"He isn't," Slater said. "Never was. Poppy's not the hunting type."

"Well, then," she said, "he didn't need a hunting knife. He must have had the knife in his car because he was a punk."

Slater had stifled a choky gulp from a sudden tightness in his throat. Poppy a punk? The association with his father was foreign and jarring. The word was still significantly insulting in those days, long before punk rock or punk culture. Until the seventies, "punk" was still defined as "a rebel or thug" and alternatively "a young man who is the sexual partner of an older man." Slater did not know what he felt in that moment, exactly, other than the choking sensation and no slight embarrassment that it had taken an outside party to conclude what was glaringly obvious. Slater faked a laugh for Beth and said, "I suppose so," but he was haunted for days by the exchange. In less than a nanosecond, the father he revered had been exposed as a punk, what Poppy himself might have referred to as a "no-goodnik." Eventually he shrugged off the notion and restored his father to his former place in his mental outlook, but he had learned that morning in bed that even one's own father was never what one thought he was, that the sands could rapidly shift, like when you stood at the edge of the sea and the waves rolled out, the slippage of the sand beneath your feet altering your perspective and leaving you for a moment dizzy.

Slater arrives at the fellowship hall later than usual for the weekly suicide survivors meeting, but Dr. Jane is not there yet. Clay, the quiet guy who drives down from Ponca City, is not present either, so Slater sits next to SueAnn, though she usually chooses to sit near Clay. Slater has the feeling that both Clay and SueAnn are intimidated by the others in the group and even by Dr. Jane. SueAnn and Clay are the only natives of Oklahoma, the rest of the group just by chance consisting of coastal transplants. Slater is from New York; Jane is from San Francisco, here on an NIMH grant; Holly came from Los Angeles to open the only bookstore in Hope Springs, other than the one on campus. He greets SueAnn, and she laughs a bit nervously when she says hello, then resumes sipping coffee from a Styrofoam cup. She wears perfume he has never noticed before, though maybe he just has not been close enough to her. Rather than the floral scent he might have expected, SueAnn's perfume smells like vanilla. He finds the fragrance more than a bit appetizing.

Dr. Jane enters the room. Slater tries not to look her in the face. The last time he saw her, she was in Siesta Sancho's restaurant flirting with a guy young enough to be her son. Yeah, well, so what if he's a bit jealous of the young man. She seems to be surviving her own grief well enough, if she can take up with a handsome youth. Next to him, SueAnn gives off a lot of warmth for such a petite woman. Though she is slightly plump, he would not have thought of her as large enough to radiate so much body heat. Maybe she's having hot flashes like Beth used to. He debates telling her she might consider knocking off the caffeine but thinks better of it and says nothing.

"Would someone like to begin, this evening?" Jane says, all business now, her "therapeutic mask" in place. Slater wonders if she showed that expression to youngblood when they were in bed together.

"I'll start," he says. The rest of them say in unison, "Thanks, Dave," sounding like the folks in the A.A. meetings held down the hall, and all eyes pivot his way. He notices SueAnn has a little gold cross on a chain, or is it a crucifix? He can never remember the difference. The thing rests on her considerable cleavage, which is pinkish, also probably indicative of hot-flash activity.

"I'm not saying this group hasn't helped me," Slater says, "but I feel like everything is backwards." No one says anything, and Slater does not know what to say either. He had not planned to speak tonight and is not sure what he's getting at. He goes with the flow, just lets the words edge themselves out.

"Just before Beth and I were married, we lived in a sixth-floor walk-up a few blocks from NYU." He looks around, sees that the three women seem actively attentive. "The fixtures in the bathroom were transposed," he says.

The women look at him quizzically.

"The faucet with the H on it had cold water, and the one with the C on it had hot water," he says.

Holly laughs. "When you said the fixtures were transposed, I had this yucky image of the toilet flushing into the bathtub."

Slater tries not to look at her legs. "As my dad used to say," he continues, "we're all creatures of habit, so of course no matter how long we'd lived there, we often forgot that the faucets were backwards and we'd either step into an ice-cold shower or scald ourselves when we tried to throw cold water on our faces."

Slater cannot find the words to express what he is trying to convey to the group. None of them speaks for a few moments, until Jane offers the hand gesture she sometimes makes to indicate that the speaker should continue: a soft little curlicue in the air.

"Since Poppy died, my whole life is like that cockeyed bathroom. When he was alive, I didn't love him enough. Now that he's gone, I love him too much. And it's the same with Beth—I loved her most of my life, but now it's like I feel nada."

There is silence in the room for a few moments, and then Dr. Jane begins pontificating about the effects of grief on familial relationships, but Slater has heard it all before.

Now Holly speaks. "Dave, have you ever read much Bellow? Saul Bellow?" she says. When Slater acknowledges he has not, Holly continues, "I read something in his collected letters. I never forgot what Bellow said: 'Losing a parent is like driving through a plate glass window. You didn't know the window was there until it shattered. But then for years to come, you're picking up the pieces, down to the last splinter of glass.'"

Surreptitiously, little SueAnn touches him on the arm, her fingers hot as a sauna. When he looks sideways at her, she leans in and says sotto voce, "I don't love anyone no more, either."

Slater walks across the quad toward his car after his nine-o'clock design studio. The students had been there overnight for a charrette and were wired from caffeine and "smart drugs" and whatever else young people use to stay awake; when he was in school, the students had only coffee and the occasional bennie to get them through the all-nighters. The sound of horns and drums erupts into the morning air. The marching band, practicing for the weekend game, is playing the song "Oklahoma!" As he heads away from the architecture building, a memory long buried rises: One year, his father had marched in New York's Labor Day parade, and from the sidelines in the crowd Slater had seen his father march right by him in the ILA drill team. Poppy had been practicing with the team every weekend for months before the parade and was designated as one of the marchers who carried and brandished a cargo hook as the drill team marched in formation. Slater was thrilled, as the cargo hook maneuvers had long been his favorite part of the parade—not counting the times the NYFD hook-and-ladder unit stopped and raised the ladder higher than the buildings on the parade route and a fireman ran up its steps and everyone cheered. Slater's mother had been pregnant again that year, which may have been why they were able to get a seat at the curb, nothing blocking their view of the bands and marchers passing by. Now Slater gets into his Solstice and slams the door shut, but he still hears the muffled sound of the marching band playing "Oklahoma!" with much swagger. The band in front of the ILA drill team on that Labor Day was playing "Oklahoma!" too; the movie had come out that year. Poppy told his family before the parade, "The minute you hear 'Oklahoma!' start watching for me at their stern."

He envisions Poppy, one arm behind his back, marching in unison with a line of union brothers also with one arm behind their backs, all with their right arms raised high, their cargo hooks slicing the air in dazzling arcs. The motions the men made with their hooks were balletic, but they also held a defiant subtext: every longshoreman knew cargo hooks had been used as weapons by union men during strike-busting attacks against them in the 1930s. It seemed to Slater on that Labor Day that his father was the handsomest man on the drill team, the one most crisply in step, the tallest marcher with the most concise slices in the air with his hook. As his father high-stepped by them, Slater's heart leapt up. He dropped his bag of peanuts to the curb in order to applaud.

Slater has to pick up an exchange student from Japan at the airport this morning. He is running a tad late, as one of his amped-up students asked for feedback after the bell rang and they lingered in the studio a few minutes. He swings the car onto Main Street, which will take him onto the turnpike to Tulsa, at the same time leaning toward the glove box for enough quarters for the tolls. Someone honks, and as he raises his head, he imagines that he sees Beth coming out of a building. The guy who honked seems to be in a hurry, so Slater does not slow down to check out the Beth lookalike, but the woman is exiting the town's Kingdom Hall. A short laugh escapes Slater's throat: Beth walking out of a Jehovah's Witness house of worship, no frickin' way. He looks into the rearview mirror, though, and damned if there isn't a silver Odyssey like Beth's parked right in front of the hall. He turns onto a side street and decides to swing back around and get a better look. He speeds up, since the woman is walking toward her car and he does not want her to get away.

Slater manages to wheel into the area behind the Kingdom Hall and still be able to see the Beth doppelgänger walking toward the Odyssey. She does not wear shorts, as Beth often does, but a white suit of some kind, a skirt and jacket he has never before seen. She opens the car door with one hand, but he can see that in the other hand she carries—not a Bible, which would be weird enough—but what appears to be a stack of those pamphlet things they call the *Watchtower*. It *is* Beth. He sees the vanity plate as she drives off: LUVNY. He is tempted to follow her, but he does not know what he would say when confronting her. And the fact is, the kid from Japan will be waiting alone at the airport and Slater is already running late.

He heads back onto Main Street toward Tulsa, trying to make sense of what he has seen, to impart some sort of logic to the incident. In any case, she's usually opening her gift shop at this time of the day, and don't Jehovah's Witnesses meet on Saturday or Sunday mornings, not Thursdays? The road in front of him swims before Slater's eyes, and he tries to blink away some unpleasant floaters from his field of vision. A couple of weeks ago in the therapy group, Clay used the term "poleaxed." Now Slater knows what the word actually means; he has just been hardcore poleaxed.

The first time Slater was aware of being a disappointment to his father was at Atlantic City. The family had driven to the shore for a summer vacation, and Slater and his parents were exploring the boardwalk after a morning on the beach. Slater remembers first noticing people pointing at something and hearing someone say, "Oh, there he is!" Coming toward them, growing larger and larger as it approached, was a huge peanut wearing a top hat. The hat added to the peanut's height and made it considerably taller than Poppy. As the thing came closer, Slater could see stippling on the inhuman shell-body.

"Look, it's Mr. Peanut," Mom told Slater. As Mr. Peanut continued walking toward them, Slater could see that he wore a monocle—what Slater thought of then as a round glass thing over one eye. The glare from the sun had the effect of occluding the eye, turning the peanut into a Cyclops. Slater was terrorized and grabbed his mother's hand. The peanut wore white gloves that frightened Slater; the arms and legs resembled human limbs, but the cloth hands seemed unnatural, spectral. The face on the peanut bore a grisly fixed smile. When the thing brandished his cane at them—Slater now knows the mascot intended only a friendly greeting—Slater lost it. He remembers howling and grabbing Mom's waist and hiding his face in her maternity smock. Mom had patted him on the back and reassured him that Mr. Peanut was a good guy, and soon the embodiment ambled away down the boardwalk.

"Let's get you some cotton candy, Davey," his mother had said, clearly trying to calm him, but his father had remained silent. Later, back in the car, Poppy turned his face toward the backseat and said, "You need to toughen up, kiddo. Men aren't afraid. Boys aren't afraid of peanuts." Slater can still see his father's expression: he had the same look on his face as when he helped Rabinowitz's father pump out the septic tank at their fishing camp.

When Slater wakes, Beth is already awake, lying on her side looking at him. Now, *there's* something that hasn't happened in a long time. Back in the day, he would often wake to find Beth propped up on one elbow, gazing at him with a tender expression and a smile, but now she usually gets up before he does and he wakes by himself.

"Why aren't you up already?" he says. He has a hard time looking her in the eye, not knowing how he can bring up the topic of his sighting of her at the Witnesses' house of worship.

She tells him she's not going to work this morning, that she has a doctor's appointment. Who knows what's true anymore? He segues away from this conversation.

"You know what I was thinking about last night at group, Bethie?" he says. "That apartment on Houston where we lived when I was adjuncting at NYU—remember that place?"

"Oh, god, yes," she says, laughing. "The studio with the bed that slid under the bathroom."

Beth's memory is correct. The studio had a certain charm to it, in Slater's view. There were bay windows, oak strip floors, crown moldings, and other nice touches. But the building's version of a Murphy bed was a mattress that slid from the wall in a tray that rolled out into the room at night, then back on the rollers in the morning to its resting place directly under the bathroom, which was three steps up from the rest of the studio. More than once they had joked about their bed's resemblance to the cadaver trays that slid out from a wall at the morgue. He says, "Remember when we first moved in, and our dining table for the first few weeks was a cardboard box?" They had sat on pillows on the floor.

"You were really romantic, though, Dave. When I came home from work, you'd have paper placemats on the cardboard box and candles lit, and a rose in a little bud vase you found in one of those trinket shops in Chinatown."

Beth seems a bit wistful, and the memories are sweet for him, too. "You had a lace petticoat from one of your theater productions that you hung over the window to give us some privacy when we made love on the window seat." Slater is grateful to Beth that she does not say something like "Yeah, back before you were impotent." He smells bleach in the sheets on their bed, and a hint of musky cologne wafting from Beth's bosom. He feels nostalgic and wonders for a second if they might find time for a bike ride this morning, or maybe a quick swim at the lake. He looks closely at his wife. Yes, he remembers the young Beth of the Houston Street days, but the woman in bed beside him might as well be a mail order bride from Russia, someone he ordered up from the Internet; he has no flaming concept of who she really is. There is no point in mentioning the Kingdom Hall sighting. She is too far gone. Or he is.

"It's odd that you would bring up the place on Houston just now," Beth says. Slater looks at her: why? "I'm moving out, Dave. I've found a condo over on Magnolia, and I've put a down payment on it."

At first Slater doesn't get it. They already own this house and hardly need a condo. But then her words sink in: I'm moving out. Now she adds, "And I'm not really going to the doctor today, I'm seeing a lawyer."

For a moment he weighs his options: talk things out, have a confrontation, kiss her, kick her rear end. But what happens instead is that inwardly he says, *Oh, well*. Or maybe he even says it out loud. They lie on the daisy-dotted sheets in silence.

Slater is aware that once you start going back to the films from your youth instead of watching the new releases, you have entered your eldership. When he was a teen, he noted that his parents stopped going to film festivals and art cinemas. When they occasionally went to the movies on a Saturday night, they came back complaining that all the films now were too vulgar or too depressing. Slater had been embarrassed for them when they went to repertory theaters to see *Casablanca* again, or glued themselves to the Admiral in the living room when *Our Town* with William Holden came on TV. Slater had sworn he would never become the sort of loser who wanted to live in the past. But here he is, sitting in the TV room of his home with a stack of DVDs on the end table, none of the films made after 1969. Beth is still in residence but has gone to her yoga class—the classes that should have been a clue months ago. He has observed that once a woman starts going to yoga classes, she tends to leave her husband before long. In that regard the classes seem to have replaced the "consciousness-raising groups" of the 1970s. Or maybe there never were any yoga classes. Maybe, like Dr. Jane, she's seeing some young stud, or maybe she is "worshipping" or "witnessing" or whatever it is she is doing behind his back.

Slater has spent the past two-plus hours with *La Dolce Vita*, always his favorite Fellini. Later this week he'll be viewing some Bergman and watching Butch Cassidy again. Mastroianni is on pause, as Slater needed a bathroom break and also stopped by the kitchen for another Sam Adams and a refill of his popcorn bowl. The all-night party scene in the film has gone on for almost as long as an actual all-night party, and he knows the ending is coming soon. When he presses Play, sure enough, Marcello and his fellow attractive degenerates are running in their formal attire at dawn from the party mansion to the beach, calling out, "What's that?" as they spot something at the shoreline.

Washed up at the water's edge is something massive, swollen and formless. There is conjecture among the partiers about what the thing is, and guesses as to whether it is alive or dead. Marcello, tottering with dark bags under his eyes, smirks at the face of the creature and sways above it on his shaky legs. Slater too is having trouble identifying the beast. Is it a ray, or a gargantuan distorted flounder? It almost seems to be a figmental being rather than an actual denizen of the sea—some Old Testament leviathan. The jaded playboy portrayed by Mastroianni stares at the one visible eye of the sea monster, their gazes locked like a nightclub hypnotist and his subject.

While Slater stares at Marcello as Marcello stares at the eye, another such orbit materializes in the foreground of his mind. He feels like he is looking into a mirror at a man looking into a mirror. There is a squid in Slater's past, a creature he knows was nothing as monstrous as the dead, bloated ray on the Italian beach, but when he was a kid, the squid he saw seemed every bit as horrific. He no longer recalls how old he was at the time, but he knows the event was at least a couple of years after the Mr. Peanut episode. By that time Mom had given birth to his first sister, who was a toddler then, so Poppy took David alone to Rhode Island one weekend that May for a squid-fishing trip. They had driven to the bridge to Goat Island, not far from Newport. It was dark by the time they arrived, but that was as things should be, because squid fishing was done at night. Slater had napped in the car on the way so he would be able to stay up so late. He had been excited, envisioning hauling in a sea creature like the grinning cartoon octopus in the illustrations for "The Little Mermaid" in the family's volume of Hans Christian Andersen tales. He had wondered if the squid would blow heart-shaped bubbles like the creature in the book and then smile up at him when it was lifted from the water, if it might have a gold crown on its head like the octopus in the storybook. He had helped Poppy carry their gear from the car: two rods, a Coleman lantern, a dip net, and their bait box and ice chest.

The view as they approached is one Slater will always remember. One side of the bridge was packed solid with fishermen, their glowing lanterns like oversized fireflies over the water. The scene was festive as a carnival, and Slater's heart thumped with the thrill of the spectacle, which at the moment seemed even more exciting than being at Coney Island. Men and boys whooped around them, shouting congratulations to each other as squids were raised in dip nets.

But as is always the case when fishing, the wait for a catch became tedious before long, and Slater grew bored and sleepy, up hours past his usual bedtime. His father told him more than once during the evening to stop whining, but finally Poppy got a hit, yelled, "Whoa, Nellie!" and began straining against his line. After what to Slater was an interminable amount of time, his father finally flipped the squid into the net and began hauling it up. Slater leaned over the side of the bridge, moving the lantern closer to get a good look at the creature. He could hear the caught squid thrashing in the net, and just as his father pulled it over the railing, black stuff gushed from the rim, alarming Slater. "He's inking us," his father said, laughing.

Not only did the squid not wear a crown like the octopus in the book, but its entire head was grotesque. The creature was gigantic and slimy looking, its face indistinct and repugnant. As Poppy hefted it into the ice chest, he said to his son, "The bugger weighs at least twenty-five pounds." Slater had hung back, frightened by the monster but not wanting his father to know. Poppy grabbed his arm and pulled him toward the chest, telling him to have a look. Urine leaked down Slater's legs and he prayed his father would not notice. Looking up at Slater was a huge, disturbing eye, not a blue eye with curly eyelashes like the one in the book, but a black, inky carrion eye, staring him down.

On the screen, Marcello observes bitterly that the creature is glowering at him. Slater presses Pause again and contemplates the screen, as immobile as the beached animal. The monster's eye stares even in death.

ASH

Behold, I shew you a mystery; we shall not
all sleep, but we shall all be changed.

I Corinthians 15:51

SueAnn starts to ring up the purchases of a regular customer, a skull-faced, copper-haired woman who, from the looks of her, is probably a meth user. But ice-lady holds up one hand in a "stop" motion. Each time the woman comes into the store, she is bonier and bonier, and her mouth has taken on the look of someone shedding teeth.

"Got any more of these ones?" she asks, and points to a can of powdered baby formula. "This is the last one there is," she tells SueAnn, her tone accusatory.

Even though SueAnn knows that she herself was no great shakes as a mother, the thought of this ice-head tending to an infant bothers her. She offers the store-mandated response: All we have is what's on the shelf. The woman coughs a rheumy cough without benefit of covering her mouth, and counts out coins, placing them on the counter, including stacks of pennies. Well, the cans of formula at least indicate that the woman is not nursing her poor baby.

How long has SueAnn hated working in the Dollar Thrift-O? She has realized a few things recently, and one of them is that even Walmart seems like Neiman Marcus when compared to her place of employment.

SueAnn sweeps the money from the counter, sorts it into the register drawer, and manages a fake-pleasant rendering of have-a-nice-day. Last week at the suicide survivors group meeting, her new friend and fellow survivor Holly stated that she was thinking of giving the clerk in her bookstore his walking papers. When SueAnn woke the next morning, the plan was as clear as a supermodel's skin: she will see if she can convince Holly to hire her for the bookstore job, which will mean she may be able to let the door to Dollar Thrift-O swing shut behind her for the last time.

"Where ya keep your Bugler's papers?" asks a man who has just approached the counter. She points to the back left corner of the store. He has an enormous lump in one cheek and an obvious can of Skoal in his back pocket. If he uses dip, she doubts he plans on rolling only plain tobacco with the papers. Does every druggie in Hope Springs shop in the Dollar Thrift-O?

She remembers now that her husband asked her this morning to pick up a tin of Skoal. She is no longer willing to overlook his habit. Before she joined the grief support group, she had not completely realized how red-necky dip actually is. Gilbert has always used Skoal, and her daddy was never without a tin of Grizzly in his back pocket, so spit cups and stained teeth have long been part of her life. A couple of weeks ago before the grief support meeting, she heard Dave and Holly snickering about all the bulging back pockets in Hope Springs, and Holly said "dip," making little quotation marks in the air with her fingers.

"I read an interview somewhere recently," Dave had said, "that claimed 'smokeless isn't just for rednecks and baseball players anymore.' Baseball has even discussed outlawing it, so guess who that would leave." SueAnn felt herself blush and felt relief that her new East and West Coast friends had never met Gilbert. She had once been proud of her husband, but that was long ago, when he was a handsome young oil rigger. Since their son died and she made new acquaintances, nothing is as it was before. As for the problems in the bedroom, she is not so sure there is any hope left in that area.

The man who asked for Bugler's returns and tosses the papers down onto the counter. "Gimme a packa Trojans," he says, smirking lewdly and pointing to the rack behind SueAnn. For a nanosecond she wishes both him and her in their coffins—caskets far removed from each other. *Forgive me, Lord*. He's a fool, though. Buying condoms at a discount store is not the greatest idea; they are close to their expiration date.

SueAnn and her husband eat in silence, the thrum of the refrigerator and the scraping of cutlery the only sounds in the kitchen. Gilbert repeatedly loads his fork with big chunks of baked ham and slides them into his mouth, looking down at his plate and showily not at her. She has become accustomed to this weekly scene, and inwardly dubs it the Wednesday Night Freeze-Out. His silence during supper is Gilbert's way of reminding her that he does not approve of her going off to the therapy group meeting. She and Gilbert will leave the house about the same time, she driving off in the Silverado, headed for the Bethel Baptist fellowship hall, and Gilbert driving the Dodge Dakota and heading toward their own church for Bible study. Why do they have to have two gosh-darn trucks, anyway? She would prefer to drive one of those cute little Nissan Cubes or a convertible like Holly drives, but Gilbert insists on American vehicles and believes anything but a truck is a waste of money.

Gilbert's voice startles her. "Last Wednesday," he says, "Pastor Russ read from Proverbs that we should always avoid bad company and not walk away with them."

It's not worth mentioning to Gilbert that he just put forth a slight misquotation from Scripture. "What are you trying to say, Gil?" She stares across the table.

"I'm *saying*," he replies, "that if you skip Bible study and instead hang out in bars with a *Hebrew* and some mackerel snapper from California, maybe you're on the wrong path."

She reminds him that she and her friends do not "hang out at bars"; after group, they have one margarita in a Mexican restaurant. "As for 'mackerel snapper,' I haven't heard Catholics called that since I was a teenager." She adds, "And *Jesus* was a Jew." Gilbert's holier-than-thou attitude about the margaritas annoys her. Sure, they're Baptists, but she and Gilbert have always allowed themselves a low-point beer or two, and even a beer-and-a-shot during Super Bowl. Gilbert says nothing.

Previously she accepted that everything in the Bible was fact, that homosexuality was an abomination, that those who did the Lord's work were assured of their rightful place in Heaven, that those who did not follow God's will and laws were doomed to burn in Hell. Now she is not so sure.

At Hope Springs Cornerstone Baptist, Pastor Russ presses extreme concepts on the congregation. He embraces the idea of the Rapture, which has brought SueAnn up short. Yes, she still accepts Jesus Christ as her personal savior, but isn't the Rapture something of a hybrid of superstition, wishful thinking, and theater? If she had wanted to join a Pentecostal church or hook up with the Assembly of God folks, she would have done so.

Since her son's death, though, she has begun to think a lot about the nature of the afterlife. Trying to envision where her son's spirit now resides has become something between a preoccupation and an obsession. Visions of the Beyond move across her mind like the crawl at the bottom of the screen on the Weather Channel. A zillion degrees in Hell today? Maybe things are as Dave believes: that when consciousness ends, everything ends, and that this nullity takes place with death of the brain. But she has been a person of faith for too long to be able to accept that particular notion of what happens at death, though in some ways such a scenario would be a blessing—for Kyle and for her. There is something appealing about just falling asleep, dreamlessly, and never waking up. The void is nothing to fear, not at all like Hell. Or, maybe Pastor Russ is correct: one will either be routed to the flames and eternal torment of Hell or ascend to be with Jesus in a paradise so dazzling we are unable even to imagine such a venue. The only place she has ever been that sounds like Pastor Russ's description of Heaven is Las Vegas. She stands, clears her plate and cutlery, and excuses herself from the table before Gilbert finishes.

Dr. Jane is late to group for the very first time, and Clay has not arrived yet, either, so SueAnn and Holly and Dave chat while they wait. Clay, a machinist who barely ever speaks and whose wife of forty years gassed herself in their car in the garage, lives in Ponca City and sometimes comes in a few minutes late from the hour-long drive. SueAnn usually sits next to him, as he is the only other native Oklahoman in the group. She and the others have already confirmed that the three of them will meet as usual for a margarita afterward, so SueAnn plans to go ahead and broach the subject of employment. She will not sidle up to the topic, but do as New Yorker Dave would and just blurt out her request to Holly: Would you consider hiring me to work in your bookstore? Her stomach pitches as she envisions Holly laughing at her or just turning her down flat, but she tells herself Holly has never acted that way and that this nerve-concocted scenario is unlikely. SueAnn has plenty of experience in retail, but she is not a well-read person like the grad student who now holds the job.

She has been inattentive for a moment while thinking about asking Holly for employment but snaps to as she hears Holly mention the *Left Behind* books.

"The lowest I'll sink," Holly says, "is to stock Rick Warren in the shop, which galls me more than I can tell you. But if H. Hemenway, Booksellers, has to file for bankruptcy, fine—I'll go there before I'll pander to the *Left Behind* crowd."

SueAnn says nothing. She and Gilbert own all sixteen of the books in the series.

Dave emits one of his scornful laughs. "I'm Jewish," he says, "so I'm not the audience for the *Left Behind* books. But then again, I won't have a Thomas Kinkade painting in my living room, either."

Holly laughs. SueAnn does not really understand the humor in Dave's statement, but she smiles along.

The door flings open and Dr. Jane wheels into the room, bringing a fruity essence of perfume with her. "Please excuse me for being late," she says breathlessly. She takes her regular chair. "I'm afraid I have a bit of bad news to share."

No one says anything, not even Dave. There is a brief silence, and SueAnn observes that Dr. Jane's bottom lip is trembling.

"It's Clay," she says. "I'm sorry to tell you he passed away last night."

"Oh, my god—he did it," Holly says, rattling the metal chair against the floor as she halfway jumps up.

Dave sits apparently dumbstruck, silent for once. He blinks rapidly.

"What happened?" SueAnn asks Dr. Jane. Maybe Holly assumes Clay killed himself, but SueAnn knows that's not usually the Oklahoma way. Clay is a man of faith. Was. If God had a wallet, he'd keep a photo of Clay inside.

Jane says they cannot be sure until after the autopsy. "Clay's daughter says he was being treated for heart failure," she says.

"That's too fucking ironic," Dave says. "A broken heart."

Jane says quietly, with a tremor in her voice, "Let's share a moment of silence." She bows her head and closes her eyes, and they all follow suit, even Dave.

SueAnn offers up a silent prayer for Clay, but Satan has his way, because selfish thoughts set in. Why couldn't she, instead of Clay, die of a broken heart? Clay was a good man who always tried to do the Lord's work and to walk in the light, whereas SueAnn feels her work on earth is done, that she just wants to be with Kyle. Loud laughter from the A.A. meeting down the hall breaks the silence in the room.

Finally Dr. Jane says, "Who would like to begin this evening?"

For a moment or two the room is again silent, save for the continued haw-hawing from the A.A. room. "Do you think we could just, you know, cancel for tonight?" Holly says. "Our own problems seem a bit trivial just now."

Before Dr. Jane can respond, Dave says, "Dammit all to hell! I was planning to ask Clay along tonight when we go out for a drink. We've been excluding the poor guy."

"David," Jane says, "don't put anything on yourself. Whether you invited Clay for cocktails or not has nothing to do with his death."

They all agree to adjourn, and Jane tells them to feel free to telephone her if they need individual counseling. Once outside the church, SueAnn says, "Shouldn't we skip Siesta Sancho's tonight?" Holly and Dave look at her, seeming puzzled. She adds, "Out of respect for Clay?"

"I think it would be good for us to talk about Clay," Holly says. "To help us process what happened."

Dave nods in agreement and adds, "Besides, after that, I need a drink, big-time." As they walk across the parking lot to their respective vehicles, Dave places his hand at the base of SueAnn's back, just above the waist, the first time he has ever touched her. The gesture is one of comfort, yet SueAnn is ashamed to realize that the heat of his hand through her blouse strangely stimulates her, a completely inappropriate response for a moment like this one. What is more notable is that she no longer feels anything when Gilbert touches her, so she is not clear why Dave's heated palm should be any different. She quickly branches off to the left to get into the Silverado.

SueAnn has some trouble parking her truck in the Siesta Sancho's parking lot. She does not wish to scrape against another vehicle as she did one day in the Dollar Thrift-O lot, which obliged her to cough up a thousand-dollar deductible, enraging Gilbert. By the time she enters the restaurant, Holly and Dave are already seated at a small table not far from the bar.

"We took the liberty of ordering for you, hon," says Dave. "Rocks, no salt, right?" SueAnn feels mildly flattered that he has remembered her preference. She nods and sits down with them.

"I just can't believe the poor guy is *dead*," Dave says, shaking his sizable head. "Now he's here, now he's not, like a puff of smoke. Crap, I wish I still smoked."

Holly says, "It's just like when Reed died. When I said goodbye to him that morning, he was alive—he looked over at me with this *look* in his eyes that I didn't realize was so . . ." She makes a little moue with her red mouth. Chanel lipstick, the shade Fire, Holly told SueAnn once when asked. "And when I got home that evening, he was lying on the bedroom floor with no . . ." She reaches for the drink the waiter has brought.

SueAnn knows the remainder of the sentence could have been "no life in him," or "no face" or even "no head." There's no way SueAnn can ask for a job now, with Holly looking dazed and ashen, her red lips like a gash.

"Dammit, we should have been asking Clay along for cocktails all this time—what's wrong with us?" Dave says. He asks the waiter for an extra shot of tequila on the side.

Dave looks stricken, and SueAnn feels bad for him. "But wasn't it because he lived in Ponca?" she says. "I mean, probably the last thing he would have wanted was to go out after group and then get home even later." Dave's yellow polo shirt is unbuttoned at the neck, and she finds herself looking at the curly chest hair that coils from beneath the garment. She cannot help but notice that there is not a trace of gray. She looks away and takes a biggish sip from the margarita. *It's nothing, Kyle— I'm faithful to your father.* Another thought creeps into her mind, one not directly addressed to Kyle. Gil had been hard on their son, bullying him from crib to casket. He had whipped him with a strap if Kyle was even half an hour late beginning his chores; he had forced the boy to sign up for the Pop Warner league, even though Kyle wanted to take guitar lessons on the weekends. Once, and she will never forget this as long as she lives, she overheard her husband call Kyle the p-word, that feline word men say sometimes, a word SueAnn had never heard Gilbert say before then. Still, she has somehow restrained herself from hurling accusations at Gil; he has enough suffering and guilt to bear.

She has taken a sip from her margarita prematurely, it seems, because Dave is now proposing a toast. She raises her glass. Dave says, "To our man, Clay, wherever he may be." He adds, "Though I don't suppose he can hear us."

"Maybe he can," SueAnn says, though she had not planned to weigh in on the topic of the afterlife. "I mean," she says, "I still talk to Kyle, sometimes. And lots of the time, I feel as if he's watching me, watching everything I do."

"Like Dr. T. J. Eckleburg," Holly says.

"I'm sorry?" SueAnn does not recognize the doctor's name.

"Oh, you mean *The Great Gatsby*, don't you?" Dave says.

SueAnn says nothing. She can see that Dave is trying to be sensitive, not wishing to bring attention to the fact that SueAnn seems not to know who Dr. Eckleburg is. "If I remember correctly—and tell me if I'm wrong," he says, "Dr. T. J. Eckleburg was the optician pictured on a big billboard in Fitzgerald's *Gatsby*. The billboard was on the road somewhere between West Egg and New York City—isn't that right?"

"Right," Holly says. "Two huge, unblinking, bespectacled eyes watching everything that happened in what was called the 'valley of ashes.'"

SueAnn plunges in. "I haven't read the book, but I'd like to," she says. "I'll come into your shop tomorrow and buy it. Which reminds me . . ." She does it; she asks Holly for a job.

SueAnn reads the afternoon *Clarion* on the sofa next to Gilbert, who has his feet up on the hassock and is watching O'Reilly on TV. Gilbert never looks at the newspaper, so she feels free to tear out a recipe for tamale pie that sounds like it might be good. After she does so, she spots through the ragged hole a lurid piece about a couple in England. Their young son had passed away, and rather than call the police or the undertaker, they put their child's body into the car, drove to a steep cliff, and jumped to their deaths from the precipice with their son's body clutched between them.

She does not mean to cry out, but once the "Oh!" has escaped her mouth, Gilbert turns his head and says "What?" in an irritated tone, and then "What!" again after she says nothing. If she were quicker witted, she might make up a falsehood on the spot. Instead she reads the news story aloud to him.

"You'd like that, wouldn't you?" Gilbert shouts, his voice shaking with rage. For a moment she thinks he might be going to hit her for the very first time. She says nothing, too stunned to respond. "That's the problem around here," he continues. "If I would have suggested we kill ourselves when the boy died, you would have been pleased as punch. That's your idea of romance. Well, I ain't going there, woman—you've turned into a dang ghoul."

She leaves the room without responding, just gathers up the newspaper and heads toward the back of the house. She goes into what used to be Kyle's room. She now uses Kyle's old desk-top Mac, so she guesses this room could be described as the "study," though really it remains her son's empty bedroom—empty of Kyle, anyway. She should get rid of most of the furniture; the room is crammed full in the way Kyle favored. Better still, she should do as Gil wishes, get everything of Kyle's out of the room and make over the space, change it to a spare bedroom or a computer-and-sewing room. Anything but a de facto and semi-funky memorial to their son.

She wants to check if there is anything online about Clay's funeral or about when and where his ashes will be scattered. But instead of logging on, she sinks into the green armchair that used to be stacked with her son's CDs and athletic equipment and seldom used for sitting. Across from her on the wall is the Kid Rock poster Kyle had hung there—the same spot where a Teenage Mutant Ninja Turtles poster had hung when Kyle was younger. She wonders what the next set of posters would have consisted of, after Kid came down. Most lads hang posters of young starlets or rock goddesses or even Hooters Girls calendars. Would Kyle have carried on a charade and displayed posters of women? She cannot imagine that he would have taken a chance at angering Gil with a poster of some matinee idol like that boy who was in the vampire movie all the kids watched. Had it not been for the confession in his suicide note, she and Gil might never have learned of Kyle's orientation—his "lifestyle choice," as Pastor Russ refers to homosexuality.

Before you become a mother, no one ever tells you about what SueAnn thinks of as the panorama effect. She has talked to other mothers, and they say they have experienced the same thing. When you look at your child, or even think about your child, you never see him only the way he is now. Your child's present self is only a fragment of your vision of him. Before digital imagery and PhotoShop and all the other technology with which SueAnn is not terribly familiar, people used to take panoramic shots of a setting from side to side; then after the prints came back from a photo lab, they would lay the photos out next to one another and tape them together to reproduce an entire landscape. She can remember her granddaddy showing her such shots he took along the coast of Japan when he was in the Merchant Marine.

During the entire fifteen years that she mothered an alive son, rather than seeing Kyle as he had been in the here-and-now of any given moment, she had seen shadow Kyles right along with him: baby Kyle in his little blue bonnet—she had been astonished when he actually said "goo goo," just like a cartoon baby—and toddler Kyle lurching in a baggy diaper and a small white T-shirt; Kyle singing a duet of "Nearer, my God, to Thee" in the choir at church with Libby Payne's little daughter; and Kyle as he had actually been at the end: a sweet, pimply-faced, irritable, touchingly vulnerable fifteen-year-old. Each Kyle stretched out in her line of vision like an accordion. Being with one's child was like being in a hall of mirrors.

She moves over to Kyle's desk and logs on to the 'net. After a few minutes she finds that Clay's family does not yet have a bereavement website. But something else has been on her mind, even though she might prefer otherwise. When she had a private session with Dr. Jane a few weeks ago, they had talked about what Jane called "your sexual dysfunction." After a bit of embarrassing talk, Dr. Jane had torn a sheet of paper from a notebook and written something on it and handed the paper to SueAnn. "GoodVibrations.com" was written there in Jane's bold handwriting. "There's nothing wrong with what we used to call 'marital aids,'" Jane said. "They call them 'toys' now, but for me, that always conjures a weird image of Tinker Toys and yo-yos in bed." She laughed while she said this, but SueAnn blushed and wished they could talk about something else. Still, she is curious.

She gets up and goes to the doorway to determine whether Gilbert is still parked in front of the TV, then returns to the Mac and logs on to GoodVibrations.com. Oh, goodness me, she thinks, this is almost as shocking as before we had the Spam filter. She has seen things like this on late night TV, too, when she had insomnia and stayed up after Gilbert fell asleep: two women in an infomercial sitting in front of a table and handling myriad "toys," some of which looked like medieval instruments of torture, and others that looked like—well, very, very large and colorful male members. There is no way on God's green earth that Gilbert would find such a device acceptable in any way. He might possibly have a stroke. Even worse, he could call Pastor Russ and suggest an exorcism. She suspects that what Dr. Jane really has in mind is for SueAnn to use the toy on herself, furtively, to relieve the stress that being without sexual intimacy for months has caused. She is too embarrassed to tell Jane that she sometimes has orgasms in her sleep, reminding her of poor Kyle when he entered puberty and she used to find stains on his bedsheets.

A vibrator on the website catches her eye. It's not as big and ugly as the dildos and some of the other vibrating wands. This one is petal pink with flecks of glitter, and the size looks nonthreatening. Plain brown wrappers are promised the buyer, and in any case she always gets to the mailbox before Gilbert comes home. But how would she pay for the thing without Gilbert noticing the charge on the credit card bill? She sits there for a moment, trying to think of an explanation. The site is called Good Vibrations, so she can claim she downloaded a song from a Beach Boys website; he would not think to question such an excuse. She scrolls past the truncheon-like vibrators with horrible protruding nubs on them; past the ones with extensions or attachments or clitoral stimulators or G-spot probes; past the Iron Maiden and the Power Thruster; past the electric devices that create images in her mind of being shocked to death while using the thing and being found in a grotesque position with the hair on her head standing up like Don King's; past the glass devices that she fears would shatter inside her and slice her female parts to shreds. She clicks on the Fairy Dust model in Tinkerbelle Pink and then clicks on Proceed to Checkout. *Close your eyes, Kyle.* Her very first erotic purchase, done deal.

SueAnn's new life begins in a week. Holly has agreed to give her a job in the bookstore, so she will soon live the life of a woman surrounded with books rather than with dollar trash in a bargain store. But the Good Vibrations toy will not be a part of that life. On the afternoon the package arrived in the mail, SueAnn went downstairs to the laundry room and opened the plain brown box. After she inserted the batteries, she turned on the vibrator, only to hear a loud grinding sort of buzz, like an electric razor or even a small power tool. The thing was loud enough for the next-door neighbors to hear and joggled her hand like a seizure. She shut off the device immediately. Her first reaction was to put the thing back in its box and discard it in the trash can. But Gilbert might find it. Worse yet, it might fall out when the garbage collectors came and roll out into the street or land on the top of the pile in the scavengers' truck. SueAnn has never forgotten the time a neighborhood dog ripped into one of the plastic refuse bags she had left at the curb, found a used Kotex, unwrapped the toilet paper twisted around the napkin, torn at the bloody pad, and left the shredded remains in the driveway for anyone to see. If she took the vibrator to a Dumpster somewhere to get rid of it, she might be written up or arrested for trespassing. She does not need any trouble, especially not now that the bookstore is about to furnish a new beginning to her life. Burying the toy in the woods is the best plan. She has already trashed the box; the Fairy Dust wand is now in a plastic bag inside an old pillowcase, locked in the Silverado's toolbox, next to a shovel in the back of the truck.

Driving westward on Highway 51, SueAnn watches closely for the Lake Carl Blackwell turnout. She knows she is behaving foolishly, that getting rid of the vibrator in the woods is not necessary, but every time she remembers that horrible buzzing noise and the sight of the big dome-topped vibrator, she feels a sense of panic.

Just as she spots the turnout, she notices there seems to be something falling from the sky, drifting like pear blossoms in the bright and blue sky in front of the windshield. She slows the truck and pushes her sunglasses up on her head so she can examine the blooms that continue to fall upon the truck as she drives along. She sees now that the falling things are not blossoms at all, but more like ashes. What sense does that make, ashes dropping from above? Certainly there are no volcanoes to be found in Oklahoma. She rounds a turn in the road and sees up ahead of her a large truck with a load in the back, and she realizes the falling debris is being shed from the dump truck's cargo, peeling off from the pile and floating briefly aloft before gravitating ethereally to the ground. She speeds up in order to examine the truck's ash heap and finally sees that the vehicle is hauling mushrooms, mushrooms that when airborne look like ashes.

There is something in the book of Exodus; Pastor Russ mentioned the story in one of his homilies a few weeks ago. Moses and Aaron took handfuls of ashes from a kiln and threw them toward Heaven. In the sky, the ashes transformed to fine dust that floated to the ground. When the dust landed, it caused boils and sores to break out on man and beast alike. Ash to ash, dust to dust, but the dust burned torment into the flesh of everyone it touched.

Last summer when Pastor Russ went away on a mission, the congregation had a series of guest pastors. One of them, Pastor Virgil, often talked about odd ideas: about mysticism and about scientific theories. SueAnn always looked forward to his sermons, but most of the congregation was put off by him. He talked on and on about the space-time continuum and time's arrow, which many parishioners found blasphemous. He said, too, that there really is nothing new under the sun, and he made a pun about "under the son." Virgil claimed that anything in the world that you could think about or imagine had already happened somewhere, maybe was happening somewhere else at exactly the same instant.

Maybe on the very day the bomb fell on Hiroshima, ashes might have fallen on a small town in Japan, far from the epicenter. Perhaps a Japa-nese woman who had also lost her only son was driving along a country road in a prewar coupé, and maybe she had even secreted in the trunk one of those Ben Wa eggs SueAnn heard about on Oprah. It might even be true that on the time-and-space continuum, these things are happening right now to the Japanese lady. The woman might be planning to get rid of the egg before her husband finds it. She could be seeing what she first thinks are cherry blossoms falling from the sky and fluttering past the car's windscreen, then thinks are mushrooms, but comes to realize are ashes, though she is not aware they are atomic ashes. She cannot know that, like the ashes Moses and Aaron tossed toward Heaven, the falling dust will sear and scorch everything it touches.